EXCUSE ME

WHILE

I

DISAPPEAR

EXCUSE ME WHILE I DISAPPEAR

Stories

Joanna Scott

Little, Brown and Company

New York Boston London

Little, Brown and Company
Hachette Book Group
1290 Avenue of the Americas, New York, NY 10104
littlebrown.com

First Edition: April 2021

Little, Brown and Company is a division of Hachette Book Group, Inc. The Little, Brown name and logo are trademarks of Hachette Book Group, Inc.

The publisher is not responsible for websites (or their content) that are not owned by the publisher.

The Hachette Speakers Bureau provides a wide range of authors for speaking events. To find out more, go to hachettespeakersbureau.com or call (866) 376-6591.

ISBN 978-0-316-49874-6
LCCN 2020949142

Printing 1, 2021

LSC-C

Printed in the United States of America

for my family
"To rehearse the stars. Hold the railing! Don't fall!"

Contents

Contents

What if we awake one day, all of us, and find ourselves utterly unable to read?
—Vladimir Nabokov, *Pale Fire*

EXCUSE ME

WHILE

I

DISAPPEAR

The Limestone Book

I only call it a book because he called it that. He said it was the greatest book ever written, and he was sorely sorry he didn't have a copy to share with me.

He was the old man who had taken up residence in an abandoned encampment alongside the tracks. How long he'd been there, no one could say. Sanitation workers found him one morning after a night of heavy snow. With his eyes hidden behind the frosted glass of his Wellsworth spectacles, his arms rigid on the chair rests, he gave the appearance that he would never move again. One of the workmen reached out and poked the figure, producing from him a sharp inhalation. Startled by this unexpected evidence of life, the men reacted by lurching backward, tripping over the gravel ballast, and falling into a heap, one on top of the other.

The stranger, obviously alive, said nothing. He didn't need to speak. He presided over the workmen like a judge, giving them the impression that within the span of a few seconds they had been found guilty and just as promptly pardoned, leaving them forever beholden to the stranger for their freedom.

Once on their feet again, they took turns asking the stranger questions. Who was he? Where was he from? Had he been left behind when the police cleared a band of vagrants from the area in December? The stranger refused to explain himself, though he did not resist when the sanitation workers lifted him by his elbows. Stiff as a mannequin, he let them carry him the few hundred yards to their truck. He made no complaint as the men fussed over him, lifting him into the passenger seat, draping him in a blanket, blasting the heat in the cab, and setting out in the direction of the hospital.

Once his spectacles had thawed, the pale green of his eyes glistened like pond water reflecting the noon sun. The black cashmere of his ragged coat—Italian made, we would learn from its label, with fine flannel fabric for the pocket bags— gave off the scent of damp fur. Between the satin of the lapels peeked a red bow tie, neatly knotted.

At the hospital he was undressed and clothed in a gown, poked with needles, infused with saline, and then added to the duties of the financial counselor, who, failing to extract any useful information from him, not even his legal name, was pleased to learn from a nurse about the existence of a wallet.

The wallet, discovered in the inside pocket of his coat, was of a vintage metal kind. Inside were more than enough large bills to cover the patient's hospital expenses. General care for the patient was ramped up. The attending physician called in specialists, and a neurologist diagnosed Wernicke-Korsakoff's psychosis due to excessive alcohol consumption—this despite the fact that no trace of alcohol showed up in his blood tests.

I was assigned to his case after the patient had been transferred to the rehabilitation facility and installed in a room of his own. It was determined that he did not match the description in any active Missing Person report. A short article about him ran in the local newspaper, but no family came forward to claim him. We assumed that he was alone and had fallen on hard times. My job was to assess his needs and place him in a permanent residence.

When I first saw him he was standing by the window. His room looked out on the frozen lake. At a later time, he would call my attention to the view, noting that between the thin ceiling of clouds and the snow-covered ice there was no differentiation. The added tangle of leafless branches along the shore reminded me of a drawing I'd once seen—I don't remember the artist—of penciled lines scrawled on a huge gray canvas.

He was clean-shaven, with a head of silky white hair cut in a side-sweep style. His suit, in a Scotch plaid pattern, looked like it was made to fit a much larger man. There was a yellow stain above the top button of the jacket. I noticed that the leather of one loafer had cracked open at the toe. I was surprised he hadn't suffered from frostbite.

He had his coat folded neatly over his forearm, as if he were preparing to leave. He announced in a voice that was surprisingly strong, given his emaciated condition, that he had been waiting for me. I explained that we weren't going anywhere and asked if I might hang up his coat. He used the word "cordially" when he accepted my offer.

I surmised from his bearing and polite manners that he was far more cognizant than the report had conveyed. I began to suspect that his amnesia was, at least in some part, feigned. My approach changed within a few minutes of conversing with him. I saw that earning his trust would be a delicate process requiring patience. He was an educated man with a philosophical disposition. Initially, he preferred to discuss anything other than himself. He wanted to know what I thought about Facebook and electric cars. He asked if I had ever been to Disney World (yes), and whether I was married (no). He was interested to hear about any books I'd read that had a lasting effect on me. His interrogation of me continued through several meetings. In this way, Guy Fraiser prepared me for his own story: only after I had nothing left to tell was I ready to listen.

He admitted at the start that Guy Fraiser was a pseudonym. He wouldn't reveal his real name. He kept other secrets, more minor, such as his age and the name of the village where he was born. He insisted that these things weren't important.

His family raised goats and manufactured a crumbly

cheese that was famous in the region; it was Guy's chore to gather the stinging nettles that his mother would boil down to make the rennet. He described how he liked to go into the mountains to search for the nettles. One day, he climbed up to a narrow shelf below a limestone outcrop where he had never been before. A mound of soft Aeolian sand offered him a tempting place to rest and take in the view of the distant sea, and he had begun to level a seat for himself when the sand gave way beneath his hand, creating an opening to a hollow interior. He dug at the hole and soon was peering into a cave so deep that he couldn't see to its end.

He went home and returned the next day with a lantern and two friends from the village. The girl, Pilar, and the boy, Matteo, were siblings and belonged to a large extended family that had made pottery for generations. Guy secretly hoped to marry Pilar, and so he put up with her older brother, though Matteo was known for his bad temper and the body odor that wouldn't wash off, no matter how much soap his mother used on him.

Though it's not exactly relevant, I don't want to leave out anything Guy told me, so I will mention that though he had known Pilar all his life, he first realized she was beautiful when he saw her standing in the village square, holding the hand of a little cousin. The two girls had stopped to watch a traveling musician play his accordion. Pilar's hair was pulled back in a single braid; she wore loose trousers colored a blue that matched the sky, and a cotton blouse, white and frothy like a cloud; her cousin wore a polka-dot dress. Both girls wore patent leather buckle shoes without socks. They stood facing the musician, listening intently as he squeezed the bellows of his instrument. Guy, who was just eight then, watched Pilar from the side and knew he would love her forever.

When, four years later, he convinced Pilar to explore the cave with him, she invited Matteo to come along. Matteo carried the pole of a broken broom to use against any bats that dared to swoop too close to them, and to smash the scorpions he predicted would be nesting in the crevices.

Matteo was a bully and a jughead, and Guy couldn't hide his resentment when the boy proved right about the scorpions. The children saw them glistening red against the brown of sand and dust, their pincers waving, just inside the entrance. Guy tried to convince Pilar to continue past them, but she wouldn't budge, not until Matteo took charge. He attacked with his broom, grinding the end of the pole against the nest. When he was done, the scorpions had been smashed to confetti.

The children pressed forward—Guy first, carrying the lantern, then Pilar, then Matteo. The dome of the cave gave them ample room, enough to stand at their full height, except where clusters of waxen stalactites hung low. The steady drip-drop of seepage echoed through the hollow space. In the rear of the cave, they saw evidence that other people had been there before them. Pilar found a piece of hammered metal that looked like a spearhead with the sharp tip broken off. Guy found a short length of rope that turned out to be made of leather.

They had grown up hearing legends about pirates who had buried treasures in caves and never returned; their three young hearts pounded hard at the thought that they would find a chest full of gold. They kicked and scraped at the floor, but the limestone was hard beneath the crusted sand. Disappointment replaced hopefulness as their efforts resulted in nothing but bloody knuckles and bruised toes. What good was a cave if it didn't contain gold! Matteo swung the broomstick, knocking Guy hard on the knee—on purpose, Guy was sure, though Matteo claimed it was an accident. Guy held back his tears so as not to reveal himself to be a coward in front of Pilar. Matteo's fury grew, his greed insatiable. He banged the broom against the wall, releasing a loud stream of crumbling stone. Guy thought the cave was collapsing around them, and he threw his arms around Pilar to protect her. His lips touched the back of her soft neck. Even as he cursed himself for putting his beloved in danger, he believed he would die happy if he died right there, with Pilar in his arms.

She wasn't ready to die and pushed him away. The limestone stayed intact above them, and Matteo, who gave off a stink of rotten eggs, howled with laughter at Guy's fearfulness. Guy was pleased when Pilar told her brother to shut up, and then he was brokenhearted when she said she wanted to leave that stupid cave and never return.

Guy lifted the lantern, preparing to light the way back toward the entrance. But then, behind a cloud of settling dust, he saw a new hole in the cave wall, opening to a separate space. He held the lantern closer to the hole and caught sight of a smear of rosy color on the slanting surface of an interior wall: a secret room—the perfect place for pirates to leave their treasure! He let Pilar hold the lantern so she could see for herself. Matteo pushed in front of her and began clawing at the hole, Guy joined him, and soon they had an entrance wide enough for the three children to squeeze through one after another.

The chamber where they found themselves had a vaguely rectangular shape, with walls slanting to a peak. The low ceiling was free of stalactites, the floor as smooth as polished marble. In the light from the lantern, the ochre color Guy had seen through the aperture slowly gained definition, revealing identifiable shapes. Circles became eyes, the joint in the stone formed a nose. Lines connected over a boss of rock into a hulking body of a bull. On the wall ahead of the bull were forms stained red, shaded with chalky white and yellow, with lyre-shaped horns, their legs tapering to delicate black hooves; in these shapes the children recognized a herd of ibex. Overhead, wings with apricot-colored rosettes belonged to a bird in flight, with a snake held in its beak.

There must have been fifty or more figures painted on the walls, preserved in the deep chamber from the destruction of time. Some of the animals bore scratched symbols on their hindquarters—a form of ancient writing, Guy assumed. What was the story they were telling? How much he would have given to know.

I slowly came to understand that this was the great book Guy Fraiser had wanted to tell me about, a limestone book made of symbols and illustrations that were impossible to decipher with any certainty, yet were rich with infinite meaning.

The children's awed silence gave way to cries of astonishment. Even brutish Matteo appreciated the import of their discovery. They felt themselves to be in the presence of something more sacred than the saint's tooth encased in a gold reliquary in the village church. These ancient pictures were older than any saint. They were as old as Adam and Eve. Maybe they had been made by Adam and Eve themselves, and they told the story of Paradise! The children had found their treasure, all right, and they wanted the world to know. They took their amazement out of the decorated chamber, out through the long passage of the cave into the open air, where they whistled and hooted with the news of their discovery as they scrambled down the slope.

"It is never enough," said Guy, sipping the tea that had grown lukewarm while he was talking, "to experience the magnificence of a beautiful thing that has been lovingly made. We must share the experience. We must cry out with joy, sound the bell, invite our friends to see what we saw and feel what we felt. Delight matters little until it is communicated."

I was picturing the illustrations Guy had described, imagining myself in his place, feeling the thrill he had felt. I was increasingly hopeful that I could persuade him to tell me where the cave was located so I could visit it myself one day. I was dismayed when he reached for his coat and announced that he had a train to catch. Where he intended to go next, he would not say.

He asked me to call him a taxi, and while we were waiting he finished his story in some haste. He explained that after he and Pilar and Matteo had roused the drowsy villagers from their siesta with their shouting, a crowd of dozens made their way back to the cave. Everybody who saw the drawings was appropriately impressed. Soon word of the discovery spread across the region. Someone set up a booth and began charging an entrance fee. Archeologists came to investigate and published papers arguing about the age of the paintings. Claims were made regarding the ownership of the cave, bribes were exchanged, and magistrates were accused of corruption.

Then the war broke out, and no one cared anymore about primitive paintings on the walls of a cave. At the age of just sixteen, Guy joined the Resistance and was charged with the task of carrying messages across the border. He went into hiding when he learned the Germans were looking for him.

"For two years," he said with a melancholy chuckle, "I traveled from town to town disguised as a girl and protected by sympathetic families, who pretended I was their sister and daughter."

Just then an aide poked her head into the room and announced that the taxi had arrived. Guy slid his arms into the sleeves of his overcoat and adjusted his bow tie.

"There isn't much more to tell," he said as I accompanied

him down the hall. For the first time, I detected a note of bitterness in his voice.

It occurred to me only after he had been driven away in the taxi that he was spending his remaining years traveling around the world and repeating the same story over and over, as if by telling he could revive what had been lost, a quixotic effort he must have known would always fail.

This is how his story ends:

When he finally returned home, he found his village in ruins. The streets were deserted except for an old man idly poking at the rubble with a shovel. Guy recognized him as the village schoolteacher. The teacher gladly accepted Guy's offer to drink from his canteen. After gulping what was left of the water, he stared into the distance with the blank expression of the shell-shocked. It took lengthy coaxing to get him to explain what had happened, but finally Guy learned that the teacher had survived only because he had been enlisted by the Allies to serve as a translator, and so he was far away when the Germans arrived. The villagers took refuge in the cave Guy had discovered, a cave so famous by then that even the Germans knew of its existence. It was easy enough for them to guess where the villagers were hiding, and before retreating north ahead of the Allies, the German soldiers lined the entrance with powerful explosives. The whole side of the mountain collapsed from the force of the blast.

Dreaming of Fire

1.

Imagine it is 1442, and we've been given access to the workshop of a Venetian artist named Michele Giambono. We find him deep in concentration, dabbing his brush on a canvas to fill in a dragon's tail drop by drop, as if he had all the time in the world. Unlike the artist, others around him haven't forgotten the little stipulation in the contract about forfeiting his payment of ninety-five ducats if the altarpiece isn't delivered by the end of the week. The whole workshop boils with nervous activity. Two assistants hastily press gold leaf on an angel's halo, while others hammer together the case that will house the altarpiece when it is transported to Fruili. Apprentices try to look busy, measuring powders and stirring little pots of paint.

The sound of an open hand hitting the side of a boy's head is barely registered. Few people hear the *smack,* and those who do just shrug and roll their eyes. It is always the same sound, always the same boy. And it is always Zusto, the assistant charged with overseeing the apprentices, who, after hitting the boy, shouts, "Get back to work, you little shit!"

This is only a rough translation of the Venetian dialect. Whatever Zusto actually shouts, Francesco understands perfectly, but he can't help himself. As Francesco's nonna likes to say, the boy was born with his head in the clouds. He will never plant his two feet firmly on the earth, no matter how many blows he endures. Dreaming is more than just a habit for him—it is a physical need. He has to do it whether he is awake or asleep.

He picks up where he left off. As he pulls a stick around and around in a little pot filled with a thick red lacquer, his thoughts return to the clouds. He imagines he is floating on a feather mattress high in the sky. He is happy and lazy and has no cares in the world...until he is alerted by a boiling, splashing sound, and the next thing he knows, a dragon rises out of the sea, exhaling a flame that is the same color as the paint. He hears the telltale crackle and smells the smoke from his singed hair. *Mamma mia,* his head has caught on fire! He dives from the heights into the sea. The dragon follows him, propelled by its huge tail. Francesco is a fast swimmer, but not fast enough, and the dragon gains on him and is about to swallow the boy whole when a giant dolphin arrives just in the nick of time. Francesco grabs the fin and throws a leg across its back. The dolphin leaps in a high arc and plunges with barely a splash, like a horse over a course of barrels. The dragon, falling far behind, roars in fury.

But it isn't the dragon roaring—it is Zusto again, communicating to Francesco that he is a lazy, rotten, dim-witted, good-for-nothing scatterbrain who has managed to spoil the lacquer, making it unusable.

"You're done," says Zusto, seemingly exhausted by his own anger. "You're not wanted here anymore." He grabs the boy by the collar and drags him across the room and out the door.

"*Na caxa,*" says Zusto in Venetian. *Go home.*

Has Zusto forgotten that Francesco doesn't have a home in Venice and lacks the means to return to his family in Treviso? The apprentices have been staying in the back room of Giambono's workshop, sharing a mattress. Now that Francesco is no longer an apprentice, he has nowhere to go.

As he staggers away from the building, he manages to plant his boot on the tail of a cat, causing it to erupt in a shriek. Francesco is full of remorse, but the piqued feline refuses to accept his apology and just trots away, twitching its injured tail.

Francesco watches it go, then looks in the opposite direction down the *calle*. What will he do now that he has lost his apprenticeship? Another boy in his situation would be overcome with despair. Francesco, however, is hopeful by nature and is sure that something good will happen to balance out the bad. He just needs to figure out where to go next.

When you are in Venice and have nowhere to go, you can hide your aimlessness by following someone else. That's what Francesco does. He follows a workman carrying a wooden bucket full of sludge. When the workman stops to dump the sludge into a canal, Francesco keeps walking, looking for someone else to follow. He spots a girl emerging from a bakery with a basketful of bread. She walks slowly, seemingly reluctant to reach her destination; Francesco walks behind her for a few minutes, until, without warning, the girl whips around and glares at him.

"Why are you following me?" she demands. Her face has a hard, beautiful, sculpted quality. Her eyelashes, wet from the mist, are like pieces of black thread decorated with tiny, glistening diamonds.

"I'm not following you," says Francesco. He resists stealing a loaf of bread as he brushes past her—he may be hungry, but he's not a thief.

Turning a corner, he finds himself behind a man pushing a cart loaded with boxes. The man rushes forward with his delivery, calling out "*Aténti!*" to warn people further along the *calle* that they'd better get out of his way. "*Aténti, aténti!*" The man bumps up and over a stone bridge, along the *rio*, around a corner. Francesco has to trot to keep up with him. "*Aténti, aténti!*" The deliveryman cuts a channel through the fog, and the boy hurries to keep him in sight. The man turns diagonally across a small *campo*, plowing between seagulls that are fighting over the remains of a squid, and sends the flock of them into the air with his cart.

He stops in the archway of a palazzo and wipes his forehead with a rag. His clothes are drenched and his trousers hang so heavily that he has to hitch them up and retie the belt before he pushes his cart into the building.

The door remains open, revealing an interior lit by a soft glow. Francesco wonders what is inside. He becomes aware of a dripping sound before he realizes that the fog has intensified to rain. Propelled by his instinctive desire to be warm and dry, he runs through the open doorway.

Alone in the entranceway, he breathes in the waxy odor from the burning candelabra. A few steps take him down a corridor and through another doorway, and he is at the edge of an expansive room full of tables and boxes and men of all ages who chatter in a language he has never heard before. Francesco passes among them unnoticed, overwhelmed by an uncanny sense of having been in the room before, in one of his dreams. Yes, he must have dreamed of a room like this, filled with hooded strangers whose sandals peek out beneath their colorful striped robes. The very foreignness of the scene is familiar to him. For a boy as imaginative as Francesco, he has two lives to remember, one from experience and one from his dreams.

He has the mistaken sense that he belongs there. Perhaps it is his confidence that allows him to move unnoticed among the strangers. He spots the deliveryman halfway up the stairs, with the first of the four wooden boxes from his cart. Francesco picks up the second box. Staggering under its weight, he manages to carry it up the long marble staircase.

On his descent, the deliveryman casts a puzzled glance at Francesco but does not object to the help. Francesco leaves the box in the hallway on the upper floor and descends to fetch another box. The man and the boy pass once more on the stairs. When Francesco arrives on the upper floor with the fourth box, the man is waiting for him. He directs the boy to carry the boxes one by one across the hall while he stands aside, looking on with folded arms, happy to have found himself a servant.

In the room where Francesco stacks the boxes are rows of desks, their surfaces tilted at a slight angle. At every desk is a man of indeterminate age, his face hidden by a hood. These aren't the familiar hoods of monks; these are the same striped robes worn by the strangers on the ground floor. As Francesco draws nearer, he gets a better look at what he takes to be canvases and sees that they contain black lines of different shapes, some circular, some straight, some bisected with other lines, some that look like snakes. The shapes are arranged as neatly as the rows of desks across the room. The men are working silently, copying the shapes from one page onto another. Some of them are biting their lower lips in concentration, others are squinting, some look bored, some are smiling, and one actually stops his work and covers his mouth with his hand to hold back a giggle.

The deliveryman clears his throat and makes an announcement to the room, in the same strange language the men were speaking on the ground floor. One of the hooded men leaves his desk and goes to the boxes. He opens the lid to inspect the contents, lifting out a small white square made of the thinnest material Francesco has ever seen.

The dreaming boy doesn't yet know, but will learn soon enough, that the material in the boxes is paper from Genoa, and the pictures being copied by the men are letters of the Latin alphabet.

2.

Today, anyone is allowed into the Fondaco dei Tedeschi during business hours. You can shop for sunglasses, designer shoes and handbags, Italian specialty foods, perfumes and cosmetics, scarves and other fashion accessories. There is a red, timber-clad escalator that will carry you up to the higher floors so you don't have to climb the stairs as Francesco did in the fifteenth century. There are also small elevators into which you can squeeze yourself with a dozen other tourists. From the crenellated rooftop, you can take selfies and look out over Venice. You will see the Frari, the Rialto, the snaking Grand Canal, the domes of San Marco. Back on the ground floor, you might want to treat yourself to an expensive cappuccino or an Aperol spritz in the café.

We know that in Francesco's day the Fondaco was used as a warehouse for Bavarian merchants, who stocked imported goods for trade with the Venetians. Less well known is the fact that the Fondaco also housed a commercial book-production business. Dozens of scribes copied manuscripts by hand, and binders sewed them into books, producing in-expensive cloth editions numbering in the hundreds, filling shelves around Europe in the decades before the invention of the printing press.

It was in the copy shop of the Fondaco dei Tedeschi where our little friend arrived that day in 1442. It was here that Francesco made himself at home, taking a seat on a bench beside the scribes when they gathered in an adjacent room for their midday meal, helping himself to bread and soup. Those who wondered about the unfamiliar boy in their midst figured he must have belonged to someone. Only toward the end of the day did the head stationer approach him. He asked him a question, which the boy didn't understand since the stationer was speaking German. But Francesco had an answer ready nonetheless. He retrieved a reed from an unoccupied desk. He dipped the reed in ink and made crisscrosses and circles that were not unlike the decorations he saw the scribes producing on their own. He was good at imitation and would only get better.

The head stationer looked at Francesco with new interest. On a blank portion of the paper, he drew two sides of a tri-angle, open at the bottom, with a horizontal line connecting their midpoints.

In the local dialect, the stationer asked, "Do you know what an *A* is, boy?"

"Yes," Francesco lied.

3.

Four years later, the robe that used to cover Francesco's ankles now only reaches his knees. He can copy any written character, from Egyptian hieroglyphs to Hebrew. Mostly he copies in Latin and Italian. He would be the fastest scribe at the Fondaco if only he weren't so prone to daydreaming. But even accounting for his tendency to pause and stare off into the distance, he can be counted upon to cover a full fold of pages, or *quire*, in a day.

He writes economically, fitting as many letters as possible onto the page, making the lines clear, lean, easy to read. One dip of ink produces a vertical line and the foot to make a capital *L,* the next line rotates into an *o.* When ink bleeds away from the letter, Francesco swoops in with the blade of his knife to quickly scrape off the stain before continuing.

Now that he can read multiple languages, he can't resist reading whatever he is copying, whether it is an inventory of dry goods or the letters of Cicero. He can tell you how much the local merchants jack up their prices, and the proper way to hold a sword. He can also tell you what Juno did whenever she discovered her husband was cheating on her. He has wept over the death of Orpheus, imagined chasing nymphs through the woods, and pinched his thigh to make sure he, too, wasn't turning into a flower.

Today, as it happens, he is copying verses about a poet's journey through the Underworld. With sunlight pouring through the high windows of the room, Francesco pictures himself disembarking from a rowboat and scrambling up a riverbank. He feels a prickle on his neck and scratches himself there, thinking he has been bitten by a mosquito. There is no mosquito. But imagine spending eternity trying to slap away insects, or slogging through a mud so thick you can't even lift out your feet! Even worse is finding yourself braced against a huge boulder, pushing it uphill to keep it from rolling back and crushing you! He can feel the sharp, uneven surface of the rock against his cheek. He must keep pushing, but he can't, but he must…

Unless, considers Francesco, he can figure out how to escape. Impossible, as long as the devil is watching over his dominion. Francesco considers: To distract the devil, one needs a temptress. What would she look like? He has never met a woman who would be entirely suitable for this, so he has to make her up. Let's see…in the boy's imagination she wears a dress the color of the lagoon at dawn, she is as tall as a bell tower, her dark curls are piled on her head like a crown, and there are…

diamonds woven in her lashes.

Francesco blinks, startled to read these new words on the page. How did they get on the paper? He put them there.

It isn't the same as forgetting a letter in a word, or inadvertently turning an *a* into an *e*. This is much worse! He looks furtively around, afraid that his guilt is visible. The head stationer has his back to him, and the other scribes remain absorbed in their work. They have not guessed Francesco's crime.

He resumes his work, relieved that his secret is safe. He rereads what he has just written. He has only to copy more of the book, and his own words will blend with the others.

Simon, who sits closest, is not much older than Francesco. Has he ever added his own words when he is copying? Francesco is suddenly sure that he is not the only guilty party in the room, as sure as he is that every human being in the world has sins to confess. Day after day, copying word for word...how could a man not hanker to add a few words of his own? It took Francesco four years to discover the thrill, and now there's no going back. He is Adam, savoring his first taste of a juicy apple, no longer innocent but glad for the adventure.

With the stealth of a spy in an enemy camp, he changes the word *ancor* to *amore*. Later, he adds a line about his nonna's delicious minestrone. Before the day is over, he has inserted letters that spell out vertically down the page, in the Venetian dialect, *Francesco was here.*

4.

He passes a full year in this manner. His handwriting is neat, his spacing even, and he has conquered his habit of dawdling. The boy is never reprimanded for staring off into space anymore and instead can be counted upon to work diligently, his eyes focused on the paper. He can copy for hours without tiring. The binders are too busy to review all the dozens of quires filled each day. The orders for new books are coming in so fast it's hard to keep up with them.

Francesco proves so capable that one day the head stationer decides the boy is ready to take on the more complicated task of copying religious texts. These are valuable books, and in their final form they will include miniature illuminations painted by some of the finest artists of the quattrocento. It is essential that they are copied accurately, word for word, in flawless script.

Francesco learns how to build up capital letters and prepare them for the rubricator, who will add color. He practices for weeks. At last, he is given his first breviary and told to pray to God to keep his copy free from errors.

Soon he is copying missals and psalms, Books of Hours, and, finally, whole Bibles.

He finds himself wishing he were a prophet and could write what God told him to write. He imagines presenting to his nonna a Bible that includes the Gospel according to Francesco. But don't think he would ever intentionally deface a holy book with his graffiti. He respects God's Word and will be the first to remind his fellows that the Word is with God and God is the Word. Francesco is proud to have a hand in preserving the Word of God, and he is not about to change anything—not even a letter...

Except...except...why, there's an obvious problem, right here in the verses when Jesus turns water to wine. It's important to remember that there were animals present in the banquet hall, dogs and cats, even a little monkey— Francesco has seen them in the paintings that hang in the churches of Venice. The animals really deserve a mention. They probably are included in other editions, and the one he is copying has mistakenly left them out. Francesco remedies the mistake and does the good deed of putting the creatures back into the Gospel.

He also adds a note about a noisy seagull in Matthew, and an octopus that escapes the fishermen in Luke. The following week, he adds his surname, Colonna, to the genealogy in Genesis. A few days later, he includes a fire-breathing dragon in the account of Joseph's dream.

How Francesco loves to dream.

He copies and writes and copies some more, dreaming all the while. The days pass in blissful peace, until late one winter's afternoon when an angry young prelate appears in the doorway and holds up a Bible, demanding, "Who is responsible for this?"

5.

Vicenzo Constantini is a bright one for sure, on the road to glory. He'll be an archbishop someday, maybe even a cardinal. He is not yet twenty-five years of age, and he has already had the honor of attending an ecumenical council in Rome. He received his education in the Praglia Abbey at Teolo, outside Padua. During the long hours he spent alone in the extensive library, he read diligently, with close attention. He proved his intelligence in a test borrowed from midrash: when the prelate stuck a pin in a random page of the Bible, Vicenzo could correctly guess the words the pin had pierced on successive pages. His quick intelligence won him a prestigious appointment at San Pietro in Venice. It is unfortunate that the cathedral is hidden in a remote corner of the city, but the young Vicenzo has made it his mission to increase the church's influence.

The young prelate's head pokes up out of his white robes like the spadix of a calla lily. He has high-arching brows and thin eyelids lined with blue veins. One of his ears is misshapen, with extra cartilage that makes the lobe hang heavily. His lips will drain to a pale salmon color when pursed in an expression of disgust. He is often disgusted, especially since arriving in Venice. He is disgusted by the waste floating along the fetid canals, the oversized rats that slink underfoot, the buxom wet nurses who let their dresses flop open, the surly drunkards who spray their urine on the sides of buildings. Most of all, though, he is disgusted by the cheap books that are for sale everywhere.

Open one of the books sold by your typical bookseller in Venice and, if you are a fanatical young prelate looking for a cause, you will be shaken to your core. Missing are the devotional verses that are meant to be studied in contemplative silence. In place of God's law as transcribed by saints and prophets are profound indecencies, unrepeatable in polite society, that hide between simple cloth covers like the pierced hymens of brides who dress themselves in virginal white. Their authors cast obscene lies as truths and fool their readers with the promise that humanity will never have to answer for sin. They call their abominations poetry, modeling themselves after the ancient gluttons who existed in a constant state of intoxication and had no purpose other than to fornicate in olive groves. Do you wonder why Venetians are such a dissolute people? Blame the books that are everywhere, and the permissiveness of a lazy government willing to let the people learn to read. Blame the Fondaco dei Tedeschi for filling the city with pornography. Blame the scribe who dared to deface the holiest of books!

Vicenzo is ablaze with righteousness, a lone crusader leading the battle against the rampant licentiousness that has infected the whole Venetian Republic. He brandishes the Bible he has brought as evidence. If he shakes it hard enough, the monkey that has been added to the feast of Cana will lose its grip and fall straight out of the pages—or so Francesco imagines as he watches, amazed and trembling, from across the room.

The head stationer approaches Vicenzo and asks to examine the Bible. The scribes stare in apprehension at the unfolding scene, many of them worryingly trying to remember what they'd copied recently, and wondering if they had made some grave mistake or indulged in a little creative writing of their own. Ink drips from the reeds held in their paralyzed hands; the drips expand into blots, ruining the paper.

The stationer reads a verse to himself, mouthing the words. The scribes look on, waiting for the verdict, and Francesco looks on with them. When his eyes meet the head stationer's for a second, the stationer gives a slight jerk of his head to the left, in the direction of the door. Francesco lays down his reed, turns the quire he's been working on facedown, and runs.

6.

He pushes past the startled Vicenzo and runs down the marble stairs and out of the Fondaco. He runs from the palazzo that has been his home for five years, disappearing into the crowd. He turns every corner he comes to, clambers over bridges and along embankments, splashes through puddles that linger in the covered passageways. He runs down dead ends, turns and runs back in the direction he came from, turns and runs across *campi*, between walls that hide gardens, through empty markets that smell of rotten fish, past stores already shuttered for the day. There is no time to follow strangers, for Francesco isn't just running aimlessly, with no place in mind; he is running from the man who is pursuing him.

It grows dark in Venice, and the boy is still running. Are those footsteps echoes of his own, or is the hunter drawing closer? Run, Francesco, run for your life!

He finds himself in a passageway that he thinks he

recognizes...the pattern of stones beneath his feet, the smell of paint, the wooden door with the Moor's-head handle—everything is ever so faintly familiar. He has dreamed of this place, he tells himself. He has dreamed of being chased by a white-robed angel of death, and coming here, to this building, and finding the door unlocked.

He grabs the Moor's head, slips into the building, and pushes the door closed behind him. The space is unlit and deserted; the shutters are closed tight. He bangs his shin against something hard and sharp, blindly gropes beside a counter, knocks over a bottle with a clatter. He plants his boot on what he thinks is a rope but is in fact the tail of a cat. The cat erupts in a howl of outrage and surprise, causing Francesco to stumble over a bench and fall to the floor.

At least he can tell where he is now. He is back in the workshop where he once served as an apprentice. The cat is the same cat whose tail he stepped on five years earlier—it didn't forgive him then and will probably never forgive him after this second offense.

Francesco looks around. He sees nothing in the darkness, but he can picture the whole invisible room. He sees in his mind where Giambono stacks the wood for the frames, lays out his pallets, arranges his brushes. On one side of the room are buckets and bottles, in the middle is a long table, and on the table are the jars with powdered pigments that the apprentices mix together to form paint.

Francesco knows better than to make his way down the long corridor to the room where the apprentices are sleeping—

they wouldn't take kindly to his intrusion. He settles under the table for the night, covering himself with a cloth tarp, trying to ignore the rumbling of his empty stomach. He falls into a restorative sleep that is enlivened by a long dream about a monkey that runs loose at a feast, stealing pieces of cake and spilling the wine.

The next morning, the artist arrives and throws open the shutters. The cat, curled on the sleeping boy's chest, blinks in the sunlight. Giambono grabs a stick of charcoal from the table. The cat gives a gaping, sharp-fanged yawn and lazily begins kneading its claws on the tarp.

"*Buongiorno,*" the amiable painter says to the cat, or to the boy, or to both. It is unlikely that he recognizes his former apprentice after all these years, but he doesn't appear startled or angered. On the contrary, he acts as if he is pleased to have company.

Francesco rubs his eyes and returns the greeting. He watches as the painter assembles his tools and approaches a square of vellum stretched on an easel. Giambono sets to work, then abruptly stops. His hand hovers in the air, and his head turns at an angle, in apparent puzzlement.

Francesco pushes away the cat and throws off the tarp. After hastily lacing his boots he joins the painter in front of the easel. Side by side, they contemplate the drawing in silence.

Giambono's commission is to produce a copy of a painting that was made by another Venetian painter, Antonio Vivarini, just four years earlier. Vivarini's *Coronation of the Virgin* has been such a success that the priest of San Pantalon wants a second painting just like the first. But the prelates should have known that imitation bores the great Giambono. He has already taken license with the commission. His drawing is less—he would say, *more*—than an accurate copy of Vivarini's paradise; it is more crowded, with figures who don't appear in the original. In the end it will be brighter, wilder, more restless and more joyous; it will convey the inevitable excitement that occurs when people gather to watch a spectacle.

Giambono has a vision for the final product, but he can't figure out how to realize it. In recent days, he has sensed that something is wrong with his preliminary sketch. The problem with the composition should be obvious, but so far it has evaded his discernment.

He pulls a portion of bread from his pocket, unwraps it, and tears off two pieces, giving one to the boy. The painter and Francesco chew quietly. Francesco looks up at the painter and sees two miniature reflections of the drawing shining in his dark eyes.

"Boy," the artist finally says, "if you were going to paint this picture, what would you change?"

Francesco, whose piece of bread is bigger than the piece Giambono kept for himself, needs an extra minute to finish chewing and swallowing.

"I would add books," replies Francesco. Of course, he would have said that about any painting. After the five years he spent working as a scribe at the Fondaco, books are always on his mind.

"Where would you put them?" asks the artist.

"Here." Francesco points to the lower left of the composition, beneath the lion's paws. "And here. And here and here and here. And I'd make sure the books are open because what good is a book if it isn't being read?"

7.

Before I continue with this story, I should explain that I wouldn't be telling it if my husband and I, both of us recently retired, had not spent two months during the last year in Venice, in a third-floor apartment overlooking the basilica of San Trovaso, in the neighborhood of Dorsoduro. One morning, a few weeks into our stay, we set out walking. Heavy clouds hung over the city, and I could smell rain in the air. We walked along the Ognisanti Canal and past the *squero* where workers were polishing a gondola. We crossed the Ponte San Trovaso and continued past the open door of the Cantine Schiavi. We stopped for cappuccino at a bar called Gilo and then continued walking. We admired the patterns of the cloth purses in the window of the Fortuny store. Near the vaporetto stop, a lone workman was pounding a thick metal rod against a paving stone.

We had no particular itinerary in mind that day, so when the sky grew darker and we heard the rumble of thunder, we decided to take refuge in the Accademia, the city's main art museum.

One of the goals I'd set myself while in Venice was to learn about drawing. While I stood for a while in front of Giorgione's famous *La Vecchia,* sketching in my notebook, my husband wandered ahead. I drew and erased, drew and erased. The final product was rough and unskilled, but I was pleased that at least I'd captured the sideways angle of the old woman's gaze.

Moving on, I went in search of my husband. When I couldn't find him, I decided he must have followed the signs to a special exhibition on the ground floor. I took the elevator and proceeded along a poorly lit corridor. I passed through multiple rooms, each one with successively fewer visitors. Eventually I found myself in the furthest gallery, alone except for a security guard slumped in the far corner, dozing on a metal folding chair.

I stood in that gallery for a long while. Among the works on display were two massive paintings by two early Renaissance Venetian artists. The first painting, a *Coronation of the Virgin* by Antonio Vivarini, was dated 1444. The second painting, by a painter named Michele Giambono, completed three years later, was intended as a copy of the first, though there are significant differences. In Giambono's version the figures have been given more expressive faces and gestures. The colors are more intense, and the canvas more crowded. The effect, the curators explained in the label on the wall, is to make Giambono's painting livelier, but less spatially coherent.

I turned back to the paintings. All at once, I noticed an addition that had gone unremarked by the curators. While in both paintings there is a lion lying by the feet of Saint Mark, in Giambono's version the lion is holding a book beneath its paws.

I looked from figure to figure and back and forth between the two paintings. It was hard to believe that I hadn't noticed the most obvious difference right away: where there are a handful of large, bejeweled books in the Vivarini painting, in Giambono's copy there are books everywhere. An ox, a lion, an eagle, an angel, saints and angels and members of the heavenly choir—they are all holding books. Many of the books are pocket-sized and appear to be bound in undecorated cloth.

There is another crucial difference. A few of Vivarini's figures hold books, but they aren't reading them. They are looking elsewhere, up toward the source of divine inspiration. In Giambono's *Paradise*, many of the books are open, and they are being read.

Giambono finished his *Coronation of the Virgin* four years before Gutenberg produced the first Latin grammar with movable type and more than fifty years before the Venetian printer named Aldus Manutius began printing books on his new mechanical press. But the books in Giambono's painting are the size and shape of printed books that have been mass-produced. Where, I wondered, did all those books come from? Why have so few survived?

If you ever have a chance to travel to Venice, you might want to make a visit to the Accademia and see Giambono's *Coronation of the Virgin* for yourself. And, while you're there, you might want to pop into Venice's sole German church, the Church of Angelo Custode, and take a look at the handful of old clothbound books locked in a glass bookcase on the second floor. These books, I was told by the guard, were said to have been salvaged from the ashes after a fire that destroyed the Fondaco dei Tedeschi in 1505. Maybe you will succeed, as I did not, in convincing the guard to unlock the bookcase and let you examine the books up close. And maybe you will come up with a different story from the one I am telling.

8.

Let's get back to Francesco Colonna and Vicenzo Constantini, whose destinies will remain inextricably intertwined. Francesco, as you know, fled from the Fondaco and the angry prelate who came looking for someone to accuse. Vicenzo, in pursuit, took a wrong turn and went in the opposite direction, running in such a blind rage that he fell and sprained his ankle. He was forced to limp back to San Pietro, where he locked himself in his room and passed the night plotting his punishment of the boy who dared to deface a Bible.

Francesco goes on to serve in Giambono's workshop for another seven years. He is given the job of putting finishing touches on a composition's minutiae; often he can be found adding words to the open books the artist has included in the painting. Whether or not Francesco is writing anything meaningful doesn't really matter, since the script is too tiny to read.

The boy is treated kindly by Giambono. Given his important role, he is spared from more beatings by the assistant Zusto, and he is admired by the younger apprentices. It would have been a good life, and Francesco Colonna might have become a fine painter in his own right, perhaps a miniaturist specializing in the illumination of books, if a certain white-robed zealot hadn't arrived in the workshop one day in 1454 to inquire about a polyptych that Giambono was supposed to be painting.

Francesco hears Vicenzo before he sees him, and he recognizes the voice with the same abrupt certainty with which he recognized the yowl the second time he'd stepped on the tail of the cat. He sees the prelate from behind, in conversation with the artist. He sees the white robes and the shaved head. To save his own hide as well as to protect Giambono's good name, Francesco hides from sight while Vicenzo is present, and the next day he resigns from his position in the workshop.

From then on, his main aim in life is to keep away from Vicenzo Constantini. And what is the best place to hide from an angry prelate? In a monastery, of course! And so Francesco Colonna boards a boat and leaves Venice for Treviso, where he says goodbye to his family and begins the long trek into the mountains. He arrives two weeks later at a Dominican monastery tucked into an outcrop in the Dolomites. After his faith is evaluated and his work experience assessed, he is approved to receive the necessary instruction to prepare him to take holy orders, and he is appointed to that most common of monastery jobs: copying books in the scriptorium.

For the next ten years, Francesco copies books, applying himself to the task with a force of concentration that anyone who knew him in his youth would have thought impossible. Over the course of the decade, he copies one thousand books, word for word. He makes no errors and adds no reflections of his own. He copies accurately, with a reverence for the original that has come to him in his maturity.

If you're an ordinary Dominican monk in the early Renaissance living in a monastery in the mountains of northern Italy, you get used to a simple existence. Your meals consists of bread, a soft Robiola cheese, and watery wine. You speak in soft voices and spend three hours every morning on your knees, in prayer. You wake long before dawn and retire shortly after vespers. You do your work in silence, drawing your ink across the page, stringing letters together to make words. In most cases, history will not remember you.

Francesco Colonna would cheerfully have been forgotten. He was happy as a monk, he felt appreciated for his work and was beloved among his Dominican brothers. But he couldn't copy without reading, and he couldn't read without imagining. Over the years, his well-nourished imagination grew strong and agile, energetic to the point of explosive restlessness, until the day came when he couldn't contain it any longer. Without offering an explanation, he put aside the book he'd been copying, found himself a bundle of paper, folded it into a quire, dipped his reed into the ink, and gave himself over to his dream.

He dreamed that he closed his eyes and fell asleep, and in his sleep he had a dream. He was lost in a dense, thorny forest. Desperate with thirst, he followed the sounds of trees breaking in a whirling wind and the echo of water tumbling over rocks. He came to a raging river and knelt upon the bank. He scooped water into his cupped hands but stopped when he heard the sound of a strange, shrill, ethereal singing. Spellbound, he let the water spill between his fingers, and he stumbled off in the direction of the music. When he could walk no further he lay down beneath a towering oak tree, licked the moisture off its green leaves, then fell asleep and dreamed of being overcome by a love so strong it felt as if his heart were made of fire.

He went on dreaming and dreaming. For months, no one could wake him.

We don't know how long it actually took Francesco Colonna to write his *Hypnerotomachia Poliphili*, translated into English as *The Strife of Love in a Dream*. There is even some debate about the origins of the book, with some scholars speculating that it was written by a different Francesco Colonna who had nothing to do with the Dominicans and instead was a rich prince from Rome. I find this theory as unconvincing as it is unsubstantiated. Who else but a cheerful monk who in his former life had copied books at the Fondaco dei Tedeschi and served as an apprentice to Michele Giambono could have imagined the strange, fantastic world of the *Hypnerotomachia,* with its forest and gardens and ruins and nymphs and monsters? Who else but a scribe who happened to have read through the equivalent of an extensive library would fill his own book with made-up words and multiple languages? Who else but a habitual dreamer would have claimed in his preface that *all human things are revealed to be aught but a dream*? Who else but the mischievous boy who used to deface Bibles would have preferred to publish his book anonymously but still signed his name in an acrostic, using the first letter of every chapter? Who else but the Francesco Colonna of this story would have written a book that is widely agreed to be impossible to read but is still read to this day?

9.

Meanwhile, back in Venice, there is trouble afoot. Books are coming out of the Fondaco dei Tedeschi as sharp as arrows from an advancing army, striking innocent victims in the heart. Vicenzo Constantini is growing ever more appalled. He pores over secular texts and inevitably finds the most outrageous blasphemies. He pores over sacred books and inevitably finds those sorts of intentional errors and additions that boys like Francesco add just for the fun of it.

As more people read, more people write. He has heard there is a widow in Pisa who supports herself by writing love poetry, a professor in Erfurt who encourages his students to write pamphlets denouncing the Catholic faith, and a theologian in Florence who has published an astrological guide. A shadow has fallen across the world; it is the shadow cast as the mountain of books rises higher and higher.

The more Vicenzo reads, the more he loses track of what should be the clear black border separating truth from fantasy. Was there really a girl who kept a sultan awake with her stories? He hates what he reads but can't shake the desire to find out what happens next. His hands tighten into fists, as if he were preparing to defend himself physically, and he goes on reading about lust and murder, torture and incest, cruelty and death.

In a fit of righteous fury, he tears the book apart and throws the fragments out the window. He feels emboldened and looks around for another book to destroy. He delights in the sound paper makes when it is ripped. All through the night, a feathery confetti falls like a gentle snow from Vicenzo's room, onto the cloister's paving stones.

The next morning he sets out early, striding across Venice, grabbing books out of the hands of their readers and ripping them apart. A little girl bursts into tears at the sight of her shredded fairy tales. A dog hops through the crowd that has gathered, barking noisily. Vicenzo marches on. Over the course of the day he tears apart dozens of books, and he does the same the next day, yet like the false idols they are, they keep reappearing, until it seems to Vicenzo that for every book destroyed, another two appear in its place, or three, or even more, spreading like a weedy vine does when you sever the stem but fail to pull out its root.

The root, Vicenzo finally discovers, is a machine that came from Germany and on its own can stamp an inked matrix of precast letters on page after page, producing hundreds of books in the time it would take the quickest scribe to copy a single short book by hand. The machine's metallic pounding echoes through the stone *calli* of Venice, where it has been installed by Aldus Manutius, who produces cheap, pocket-sized books, just like the books that were being copied so efficiently at the Fondaco dei Tedeschi.

The printer Aldus, as it happens, learned everything he knows about books in the same place where Francesco Colonna once worked—the commercial scriptorium in the Fondaco. And when he gets ahold of the book Francesco has written at the monastery, Aldus not only publishes it but has it decorated with beautiful woodcuts. He makes such a beautiful book that soon everyone has heard of it and wants a copy.

Alone in his room with the *Hypnerotomachia Poliphili*, the pages barely visible in the light from a single, sputtering candle, Vicenzo feels himself falling, hurtling head over heels through the infinite darkness. He cries out for mercy. If he needs proof that he is blessed, he gets it when God's loving hand reaches out to catch him, lifting him into the sky. He beholds the scorching sun and then, inside the fringe of flames, a future that takes shape amidst the burning white.

It is inevitable that after spending so much time reading

about dreamers, Vicenzo Constantini would end up stuck in his own dream. He dreams that he is falling again, and this time, instead of landing in the palm of God's hand, he falls all the way to hell. He dreams that he lands unharmed, sinking into a soft bed of ashes. He digs his way out and stands facing a bonfire as big as a mountain, fueled by paper covered with words that never should have been written.

Vicenzo finds a stick and touches the tip to the fire to set it alight, then he makes his slow ascent out of hell and back to his lonely room, where that maddening book by Francesco Colonna lies open on the desk.

History will remember Francesco Colonna and his book, but it will not remember the principled Venetian prelate who stole through the *sestieri* of the sleeping city, a burning taper in his hand. And though history won't let us forget that the Fondaco dei Tedeschi as we know it today was rebuilt after burning to the ground in 1505, it will fail to mention the cloaked figure who pried open a window in the middle of the night, climbed up to the storage room in the attic, and thrust his taper into a pile of books. There is no way history could tell us who set the fire that destroyed the Fondaco, because through the rest of the night and the next day, while the fire continued to burn out of control, Vicenzo Constantini hid himself among the crowd of spectators, his pale lips pressed tight, keeping his dirty little secret to himself.

The Knowledge Gallery

I.

"You saved nothing?" I asked, unable to contain my disappointment. I'd been hoping that a woman of her advanced age would have a diary or two in a drawer, maybe index cards or even notes scrawled on the backs of those old envelopes used for baronial cards.

She idly tapped the tassel on the window blind to set it swinging. "My dear, multiply two by zero and it would be nothing. Which differs from the anything I presume you are asking about, and which, yes, the last went into recycling when I moved here."

"You have no manuscripts anywhere? No letters?"

She observed me, then lifted her head to direct her gaze

downward, through the bottom half of her bifocals. "I see you're writing with a pen. On paper. The old-fashioned way. But surely you haven't forgotten that until quite recently, paper was discouraged as an indulgent, poisonous consumption. The taxes on a single ream…who could afford it? And if you could afford it, you didn't want your enemies to know. My generation was particularly suspect—thus the public statute requiring accreditation from EcoGreen before we could receive social security. Writers, of course, were notorious. Have you heard of Olivia Gastrell?"

I scribbled the name, adding it to a list that was growing ever longer with each writer I interviewed. "Gastrell—with two l's?"

She reached for a glass of water on her bedside table and took a sip. "You haven't read her? Surprising, given your interests. She came late to fiction, published her first novel, *Fortunate Odyssey,* when she was fifty-two. She would have won a Hermes with *Say What You Mean,* but she skipped the ceremony and thus forfeited the award. Not that she needed honors to buck her up. My dear friend Olivia. She was nearly eighty when she hired movers to transfer her papers to a storage unit. Two hundred and five pounds of cellulose pulp— that was two hundred pounds over the personal legal limit. The movers were obligated to file a report. The authorities seized and destroyed everything. She had to pay a fine….I don't remember how much, but it was significant."

"Is she still alive?"

She sucked in her lips as she considered her response, then

looked toward the door, seeming to will the interruption that came a moment later, the sharp knock startling me to the point that I bounced up from my seat, then fell back.

"Come in!"

The nurse, a bearded man lithe as a dancer, entered holding a paper cup. "M&M time!" he announced, rattling the pills deposited inside the cup. "You need more water, hon?"

"I have plenty, lovey, thank you." She picked out the pills and tossed them both in her mouth, then made a show of taking a swig of water from her glass. "This young lady has come for a chat. So if you'll excuse us..." She nodded in the direction of the door.

The nurse hesitated. "You'll let me know if you need anything?"

"Absolutely, sweetheart. Now go, shoo, shoo." She waited until he had closed the door behind him, then leaned over, opened the drawer of her bedside table, and extracted a box. Cracking the lid, she removed the two pills from her mouth and added them to a substantial collection of pills in the box. "Don't tell," she said. Her imperious smile was clearly aimed to remind me that I was a minion beholden to her goodwill. "Now where were we?"

"Olivia Gastrell."

"Ah, yes. She once told me that she had an ancestor who chopped down a mulberry tree that was said to have been planted by William Shakespeare. To this day, the name Gastrell is banned in Stratford-upon-Avon."

"And Olivia, is she—"

"Fort Worth. I'll let her know you're coming." Suddenly her gaze was harsh, boring into me, daring me to react. I didn't know what to say. I was embarrassed and resentful at being forced into extending my inquiry yet again. Didn't she realize that I was there to preserve the reputation of Eleanor Feal? But in the evasive manner that I'd come to realize was typical for the writers I'd tracked down so far, Eleanor Feal didn't want to tell me about herself. She wanted to tell me about Olivia Gastrell.

It was the same outcome, interview after interview. I aimed to reconstruct a writer's work from scratch but ended up being directed by each of them to the beginning of someone else's story. After six months and twenty-seven separate interviews, I had failed to recover a single book.

II.

There was a welcome coolness in the breeze that skimmed the river. As I crossed the pedestrian bridge, I saw the sleek back of a beaver swimming toward the shore, pushing a newly felled branch that looked like a rack strung with pieces of green silk. In the shallows, a magnificent heron stood patiently, as if awaiting its delivery. The beaver drew nearer, still pushing the branch, changing its course only at the last moment, swimming upstream to some other destination.

I leaned against the iron rail and watched for several minutes. The heron remained stock-still, the current swirling around its legs, its yellow eye unblinking, the blue plume extending from the back of its head like a pomaded spike of hair. I was hoping the bird would rise into the air—I wanted to see the slow beat of its wings as it flew overhead. But it just stood there, so I walked on. Hearing a splash, I turned just in time to witness the heron lift its dripping head from the water and with a deft movement drop the fish that had been clamped in its beak headfirst into its gullet.

There in the heart of the city, the natural world was thriving. Along the path curving across campus, chipmunks scampered ahead of my footsteps. It was early May, and the air was redolent with the fragrance of the lilacs. Petals from the magnolias flitted like butterflies in the breeze. The sun, as if summoned by the carillon chiming in the tower of the Knowledge Gallery, peeked shyly out from behind a flat-bottomed cumulus cotton ball.

I was in good spirits that day, contemplating the lovely campus and the equilibrium of a planet that had fully recovered from its long fever. The climate was healthy again, thanks to the ingenuity of our scientists. We were like angels dining on wind and light and water. Life itself seemed infinitely renewable.

I was sorry to have to go inside, but I had research to do, and the Knowledge Gallery was scheduled to close early, as it often did, for a special administrative function. The building, a five-story former library with sloping floors that spiraled around a hollow interior, seemed to be more useful as a party house than a location for scholarly research. Still, the resources were vast, with thousands of databases that could be accessed by anyone with a VPN account. Numerous work spaces were furnished with whiteboards, televisions, self-service espresso machines, and more Macs than there were students enrolled in the university.

If the Gallery had one acknowledged problem, it was the noise. Most of the work spaces opened up to the echo chamber of the central gallery. From the main floor, you could easily hear the conversation of people on the fourth floor. On a given day you might hear biology students comparing lab results, research advisers explaining how to modify a search, two young lovers setting up their next date. And you could always hear hundreds of fingers *tap tap tap*ping on keyboards.

After a year as a graduate student on campus, I'd found a relatively quiet space at the back of the Rare Books Department, behind the cases used to display simulated manuscripts. Most of the furniture in the building was manufactured with repurposed metal or plastic, but in the Rare Books Department there were four beautiful antique tables made of oak. I loved the earthy smell and the rosy heartwood grain of those tables. And I appreciated the serenity of the department. Few visitors came to see the simulations, since everything in the cases was viewable in more detail in online exhibitions.

On this particular day I was verifying references for the second chapter of my dissertation and hoped to start assembling notes for chapter three. My subject was Avantism—a recent literary movement based in the US. Focusing on six writers who identified themselves as Avantis, I intended to argue that Avantism had its roots in once popular fiction of the early twentieth century and drew especially from the work of a little-known Spanish writer named Vicente Blasco Ibáñez.

In terms of its basic elements, Avantism was as diverse as literature itself. There were mysteries, tragedies, farces, fictional biographies, and biographical fictions. One novel used an encyclopedic structure, with chapters arranged alphabetically by subject. Another built its narrative out of a collage of quotes taken from other Avanti texts. Some were set in an apocalyptic future, when civilization had deteriorated into either anarchy or tyranny, and their plots involved characters struggling with the most basic hardships—there were famine and flood stories, homesteading stories set in harsh lands, stories about superflus and climate change, and stories about the total devastation of a final world war. All of the manuscripts were handwritten. Finished books were produced by expert letterpress printers on pearlescent wove paper, with painted cloth bindings.

What united the Avanti authors, besides the care they took with the printing of their books, was their love of spectral manifestations. All the Avanti novels I'd read, plus those I knew of through hearsay, included at least one ghost.

The Avantis prided themselves on scorning publicity. They had no websites, sent no tweets, and were rarely photographed. Their work appeared only in hard copy. Once all publications became electronic, the Avantis refused to publish at all, sharing manuscripts only among themselves. The general public was indifferent. By the time I'd narrowed down the subject of my dissertation, few people had ever heard of the Avantis; fewer still had read any of their books.

As a scholar of Avantism, I had to be a clever detective. I was constantly testing the strength of various search engines against the defenses of the Avanti writers. They'd resolved to hide themselves from scholars. I was determined to write their history. By then I'd spent two years on research and had a fellowship that would support me for two more years. In the end, I hoped to have a notable dissertation that would secure me enough interest from foundations to fund a Web appointment as a digital humanities scholar.

I was twenty-five years old and confident that all was going according to plan. I agreed with my peers that we were living in a golden age. The world was at peace. Every question had an answer...until the morning when I was typing the final sentences of chapter two of my dissertation on my laptop, writing the words—

What words? Maybe something close to these words I'm writing now, surely involving dependent clauses, nouns, an article, an adverb, whatever, I'll never know, because I can't remember the specific words, only the experience of watching the loop of a *b* break away from its stem, an *o* dissolve, an *a* sink to the bottom of the screen and disappear, replaced by symbols: ⊆Σφℜξω, and on and on in a blur where there had once been sentences.

III.

I was the second student in line at the Question & Information desk on the ground floor of the Knowledge Gallery. While I stood there waiting my turn, I noticed that the letters on the digital sign above the desk had been replaced by a video of cascading roses. Naive as I was, I didn't connect the roses to the symbols on my laptop screen.

The first student was an undergraduate woman whose PowerPoint had frozen—a coincidental glitch that the techie, himself an undergraduate, managed to repair simply by turning the student's tablet off and on again.

"Hi," he said to me. He had a scruff of a beard, icy blue eyes, and a bowl of donut holes next to his Mac. "What's up?"

I tried to contain my panic. "It looks like I just crashed. All my files—I can't…I mean, I can access them, but everything has been scrambled."

"Let's take a look."

I opened the laptop and touched the screen to activate the light. The symbols were still there, a wallpaper of shapes that reminded me of snorkeling: sea grass waving, jellyfish drifting, minnows darting away from my submerged hand.

"Cool," said the techie.

"Can you fix it?" I implored.

"Mmmm." Still staring at the screen, he reached for the bowl, blindly fumbled for a donut hole, and popped it in his mouth. He chewed in concentrated silence, pressing various keys and studying the screen for the results that didn't come.

While I waited, I reminded myself that a crash was no more than an inconvenience. With every file automatically saved to the Cloud, everything could be recovered. Still, it would take time to restore the files to my hard drive, and more time if I had to buy a new computer entirely.

The Q&I desk was positioned at the rear of the ground floor. It was early, and workstations still had empty chairs. But among the students scattered throughout the Knowledge Gallery, a new kind of sound emanated, a flurry of murmurs and exclamations competing with the rattling of keyboard taps and the burbling of espresso machines.

"Oh just, what, you gotta be kidding!" said a boy loudly from across the room.

"Shit, shit, shit!" cried someone from a cubicle on the second floor.

I heard chairs scrape along the laminated floors. I heard a phone buzz and then a thump I couldn't identify but sounded like a small bird flying into plate glass. I looked toward the nearest window. The sun was still shining, the magnolia blossoms still dancing in the breeze. At the Q&I desk, the techie tapped my keyboard with impressive speed, then stopped and studied the screen.

"I don't really understand why they call them holes," he said at last.

"What?"

"If it were up to me, I'd call them centers." I realized he was talking about the donut holes only when he offered the bowl to me, inviting me to take one. "I mean, the holes are what they leave behind, not what they are. It's like saying they're an absence. Identifying them with the space they once filled."

I wanted to say something insulting, but the rest of my day depended upon this techie's ability to recover my files. I needed his know-how, as did the students who were lining up behind me.

"A hole is a hollow space in a solid body." He tapped the Escape key several times. FaceTime on his Mac rang. "Hang on, will you?" he said to his screen. "On the other hand, there are black holes, defined by such a strong gravitational pull that no matter can escape. They're interesting, don't you think?"

The phone in his pocket buzzed. He looked at the number and answered briskly: "Yeah, yeah, get Daryl down here, maybe Inez, too. Looks like a busy day ahead of us." He clicked off the phone and rested his chin in his hands, studying his own Mac. He poked at the touchscreen, cocked his head to cast a sideways glance at my laptop, then shut his eyes for a long moment, as if giving up the effort to hide his boredom.

"Frankly, I don't know what's going on," he finally admitted.

"What do you mean? You can't fix it?" I asked.

"You have a Cloud account, right?"

"Yeah, of course."

"Then you're safe," he assured me.

"No she's not," said the boy behind me. "The Cloud is saying text files are inaccessible."

"My life is over," said a girl wearing cutoff shorts and a vintage Minnie Mouse T-shirt, marching toward us without bothering to take a place in line, her flip-flops angrily slapping the floor. "I give up."

"You're cutting," another girl called from the back of the line.

"Look there—" The boy behind me directed our attention to the television on the wall. The supertitles at the top of the screen were garbled symbols; the bottom strip, where breaking-news headlines usually circulate, was blank. The sound was on mute, but we could see that the newscaster had stopped talking and was looking frantically in the direction of the teleprompter.

"Must be a malware offensive," said the techie, popping another donut hole into his mouth. "We'll have to wait for quarantine mandates and the updated firewall. Everyone got the same problem?" More students were arriving in search of help. The line was long and getting longer, with students groaning, complaining, jostling one another, reminding friends about the dance on Friday in the Field House. "Hey, guys," called the techie to the crowd. "Everyone got a problem with text?" There was agreement, cursing, and laughter in the crowd. The techie interlaced his fingers, cracking his knuckles. "Come back in five," he said to us. What did that mean? Five minutes? Five hours?

It would take a good five hours for most of us to become aware of the vastness of the attack, and five days or more to understand the extent of the loss: everything written in

English, new and old, every book that had been scanned (and, as was protocol back then, discarded), every document in a digital archive, every email and text, everything involving the digital transmission of words, everything that provided our civilization with a record of its vast knowledge was gone, dissolved by a virus that had been lying latent in software from the beginning, programmed fifty years in advance to explode all at once, leaving only shreds of meaningless shapes floating with malicious wantonness on screens of English-speaking users around the world.

Luckily, the important diagrammatic programs that keep the infrastructure running, along with images and videos, were untouched by the attack. I suppose this might explain the current blasé attitude about it all. There's general consensus that the essential documents have been recovered, some located as rare hard copies, most supplied through translation. The American public has long since stopped fretting over missing materials. But let's not pretend that we've restored the full inventory. Not even close. We can't begin to know what we've lost. All we can do is keep searching, and advocating for funds for the National Archive Project. Where would we be without the NAP?

I'd be without income, for starters. If I weren't an NAP agent, I'd be unemployed. Truly, I'm thankful for the paycheck, but I also believe in the worth of the mission. This whole project is about memory. By remembering, we can avoid repeating the mistakes we made when we considered ourselves ingenious and invulnerable.

IV.

NAP Recovery Record: catalogued July 17, 2052

1) *Treatise on How to Perceive from a Letter the Nature and Character of the Person Who Wrote It,* author unknown, 1622: translation.

2) *The Queensberry Rules,* London Amateur Athletic Club, 1867: found document, complete.

3) *Epistle to Posterity,* Petrarch, 1351: translation.

4) *With Americans of Past and Present Days,* J. J. Jusserand, no date: found document, incomplete.

5) *A Tutor for the Renaissance Lute,* Diana Poulton, copyright page missing: supplied by owner.

6) *Book of the Prefect,* author unknown, 950: translation.

7) *Songs of Experience,* William Blake, 1794: translation.

8) *Horse Shoe Robinson,* J. P. Kennedy, 1835: found manuscript.

9) *Gazette,* Rhinebeck, NY, 1947–1949: supplied by municipality.

V.

And lastly, No. 10, which I failed to supply but should have consisted of a summary of Eleanor Feal's first novel, as transcribed from our interview.

"You must talk to Olivia in person," she was saying. "Her work is difficult to describe."

Courtesy kept me from pointing out that I'd come in search of books written by Eleanor Feal, a writer whose existence I'd learned of only in my previous interview with the author Timothy von Patten, himself unknown to me until the prior interview with Leonard Dumaston—and so on.

"She was an Avanti?"

"Of course. Any writer worth the time it took to read was an Avanti."

Six months earlier, I had set out with half a dozen Avanti writers to track down. The list had grown to include twenty-seven other lesser-known writers who, I was told, were not at all of lesser merit. That I had overlooked them when I'd been researching the movement for my dissertation now seemed inevitable. Avantism was an elusive prey, with its cohorts keeping a low profile. Like nocturnal animals, they spooked easily and melted into the nearest burrow when threatened, disappearing before they revealed much of anything about themselves, camouflaging their work with the work of a fellow author, as the centenarian Eleanor Feal was doing with Olivia Gastrell.

As far as I knew, all the Avanti books had been confiscated, scanned, and shredded over the preceding fifty years—there were no extant copies left in the world. I was still hopeful that someone somewhere would reveal a secret library. New recovery laws protected book collectors from the criminal charges they would have faced in the past, but no one had come forward with any valuable inventory. In the absence of an actual book or manuscript, I could at least provide a detailed recounting of the work that had once existed—this was the purpose of my interviews. But Avanti writers didn't appear interested in their own work. They wanted to talk about the books by their friends.

"Take Olivia's *Say What You Mean*—a central text for the rest of us," Eleanor Feal was saying. "It tells the story of a young woman..." She studied me, squinting, as if searching my face for a minute blemish. "She had green eyes," she said. "Yes." Her satisfaction suggested that she'd solved a difficult equation. "Like yours, the same shade." How could she be so sure? She was speaking of a fictional character as if she'd met her in person, and comparing her to me. Her scrutiny was making me increasingly uncomfortable. "A literary scholar, as it happens." I was beginning to wonder if she was using me as a model to fabricate the supposed main character in Olivia Gastrell's book. "Her name was Juliana. She finds herself living in a time much like ours, after the entire written record of civilization has been wiped out by a computer virus. In the contest of prescience, Olivia wins, hands down. Our young heroine takes it upon herself to...Come in!"

I hadn't heard a knock, but there was the nurse again,

standing in the doorway with a wheelchair, ready to escort Eleanor Feal to the dining room.

"Yumtime!" he said.

"Already? But we were having such nice conversation. I'm sorry, dear. They don't like it if we're late for meals around here!" She was suddenly cheery. "They aim to keep us in tip-top shape, you know, on schedule and such! The longer we live, the more federal funding they receive, isn't that right, lovey?"

The nurse concurred. "It's a win-win," he declared. "*Andiamo!*"

I stood aside as she lifted herself into the wheelchair the nurse had slid toward the bed. In her eagerness to be done with our interview and take her place at dinner, she seemed transformed—deceptively so. She struck me as a woman versed at playing the part of a beloved grande dame who enjoyed being tenderly cared for. In reality, she was a woman who clearly preferred to take care of herself.

"What happens to Juliana?" I demanded, following the nurse as he briskly wheeled Eleanor Feal out of the room and up a carpeted corridor.

"You'll have to ask Olivia," she said, lifting her hand above her shoulder, bending her fingers in the shape of a python's flat head to signal a wave goodbye, a gesture that had a strange, chilling finality, as if scripted to bring an end to the whole story—this story, I mean, the one I've begun but will never finish, its incompleteness I could have predicted before I asked my first question.

I gave up trying to keep up with them. As I stood watching the nurse roll Eleanor Feal down the corridor, I thought about the pills she had secreted away in that box in her bedside table. I thought about the stepping-stones of my interviews, from one Avanti writer to the next, that had led me here. I wondered about the cost of a round-trip fare to Fort Worth. I thought about *Say What You Mean,* by Olivia Gastrell. How could I be sure that it had ever existed? I wondered about all the other books that I would never read.

Thank Ye, Jim Bridger

The fur trapper emerges from the shade of the pine forest into the open bowl of a valley. He hasn't eaten since dinner last night, and he is glad to anticipate his next meal among the herd of bison grazing in the meadow. Later, he will claim that the bison were as tame as cattle when he walked among them, that he came so close he could hear their teeth ripping the grass, that one sweet calf even let him run his hand over the blond fur on its back.

Only when he cocks his rifle does the herd take notice, and then the stampede that follows seems to progress in a languorous, nearly soundless fashion, reminding Jim Bridger of pictures in a zoetrope that is being turned too slowly. He takes aim and fires. A young bull buckles instantly, diving horns first into the grass. The rest of the herd continue their lazy retreat, leaving Bridger to his kill.

He makes camp on the bank beside a shallow, twisting thread of water he names Tangled Creek in his mind. He builds a fire, spears the tenderloin he carved from the animal, and turns it patiently in the flame, giving it a good black crust. To warn away wolves and grizzlies that are sure to be drawn to the carcass, he keeps his fire burning through the night. He rests contentedly, drifting with the clouds in and out of sleep.

By morning, buzzards are circling overhead, and the eyes of the bison are thick with flies. Bridger douses his fire, straps on his pack, shoulders his rifle, and sets off in a northeasterly direction. He follows Tangled Creek for two days, turning this way and that. The grasslands give way to sagebrush, the sagebrush to fir trees that grow a hundred feet high and cover the earth in a layer of soft needles.

Along the slopes of the foothills in the distance, the forest is interrupted by bald patches of limestone. Soon the creek disappears beneath the rocky ground. The stench of sulfur in the air grows stronger. Natural limestone cones, wrapped in velvety moss at their base, striated with yellow and tipped in crimson, look as if they've been molded by human hands. From the distance, a strange rattling sound can be heard. Bridger is reminded distinctly of wagon wheels turning along a gravel trail, though of course there are neither wagons nor trails for hundreds of miles. As he draws closer to the sound, the rotten stench intensifies.

Empty craters pock the earth. The air becomes hot and misty, and Bridger feels a rumbling sensation beneath his feet.

Being by nature a man who always has to see what is around the next corner, no matter the peril involved, he presses forward between the limestone formations. He finds himself supported by a rim of rock as thin and transparent as ice. A cloud of hot steam spews from a crevice in the basalt wall.

Is this the entrance to the underworld? Even Jim Bridger knows better than to try to find out. He decides to call the hot spring Hell's Broth, a name that is destined to be replaced since Jim Bridger, being illiterate, never writes it down.

With so many natural wonders to discover, how can a lone explorer keep track of them all? He has a good, reliable map in his mind and so will be able to guide future visitors, but that is of secondary importance. His primary motive is to see what has never been seen before. And since he can't go to the moon, he is drawn to this unexplored corner of the western wilderness, where not even the indigenous tribes dare to go.

It is his first time in the corner of the wilderness that we will come to call Yellowstone. He has been traveling alone for two months by now. It will take him another ten days to cross the hills and ascend the ridge that bounds the valley on the north. He has left the herds of bison far behind. He survives on trout he catches by hook and line and a rabbit he nearly steps on in a clump of wheatgrass. He tracks a mule deer to the shore of a small lake but loses it when a strong whirlwind blows dust into his eyes. The deer runs off, zigzagging down the precipitous slope before Bridger can shoot.

He camps near the lake, which he names Lake of the Wind. Despite his empty stomach, he sleeps deeply. When he wakes the next morning, the water is covered with a thin layer of wrinkled ice, and a feathery snow is falling.

Bridger understands that he is running out of time—he has to reach the mining camp at Cooke City before the snow makes the terrain impassable. Still, he relishes the mix of fresh coolness and the warm currents of sunshine that break through the clouds. He walks briskly, humming the tune of a song whose words he's forgotten but that still makes him feel cheerful. Distracted by the sound of his own voice, he fails to pay attention to his surroundings and does not notice how the landscape is changing until the song has ended.

He looks around him. The rock formations have darkened from a sandy brown to a smooth black that sparkles in the sunlight. Ahead, within the short distance of a stone's throw, stands a magnificent elk. The elk holds its head so high its antlers threaten to poke holes in the blue dome of the sky. The animal stares straight at Bridger, unafraid. Bridger takes aim and fires. The shot and its ricochet echo in the silence. The animal does not move. Bridger looks around instinctually to make sure no one is present to laugh at him for his poor aim. He is glad that his reputation for expert marksmanship will remain unsullied. He fires again, with renewed confidence, but again the bullet goes astray. How can it be? The elk stands unperturbed even when Bridger moves toward it. One step further and Bridger will be close enough to reach out and grab the animal by an antler and might have done so if his fist hadn't banged hard into a translucent wall.

He runs his fingers over the surface. The barrier, as high as a four-story building, has the texture of obsidian but the transparency of glass. Either it is some sort of immense igneous protrusion that crystallized eons ago, or the air itself has congealed and hardened.

Jim Bridger stares in wonder at the wall. He walks in a daze, dragging his hand along the glassy surface until he finds a break that forms a narrow archway. He tells himself that if Hell's Broth was the entrance to the underworld, here is surely Heaven's Door, left open for his convenience.

He slips through, leaving reality behind. On the other side, he knows immediately that he must change the way he thinks in order to make sense of something that has no precedent. His capacity for disbelief is as suspended as the motionless cascade that spills like sculpted ice from a precipice into a river that does not flow. Stalks of oatgrass do not waver in the wind. Violet capsules of a larkspur remain half-open, stopped in midbloom. Two bear cubs are caught in the midst of their playful wrestle for all eternity. A raven overhead hovers with its wings spread, held in mid-air in motionless flight. The elk Jim Bridger tried to shoot stands as still as a stuffed trophy. Across the valley, between the wall and the opposite ridge, nothing moves, nothing breathes, yet nothing has decayed. The sun and moon shine simultaneously, with petrified light.

* * *

Did this really happen? Does this place exist? I'm not sure. During the many expeditions he went on to lead across Yellowstone, Jim Bridger liked to tell the kinds of stories that no one believed. Still, he went on telling, he couldn't help himself, and the hunters and mapmakers and thrill-seekers sitting around campfires went on listening. I'm guessing that Bridger added some embellishments with each retelling. My hunch is that he lost track of the difference between what had actually happened and what he'd made up for fun. His friends labeled him a teller of yarns, his critics called him a liar. It was understood that any newspaper editor who printed Bridger's far-fetched tales would be laughed out of town. When one impatient woman asked him why he insisted on saying things that weren't true, he replied, *There's no harm in fooling people who pump me for stories and don't even say thank ye.*

Do you blame him? What if you were alone in the uncharted wilderness, and you found yourself in the same place where Jim Bridger arrived that September day in 1830? What if you passed through an opening in a glass wall and arrived in a corner of the world where time had stopped? Would you wonder, as Bridger did, if you were hallucinating, and then conclude, as he did, that you were very much alert? Would you then decide, as the awestruck Jim Bridger did, that the valley you've stumbled into was not meant for mortal eyes and so must stay hidden from the rest of humanity? Would you go on to tell everyone you meet about this sacred place and yet refuse to reveal its actual location, bypassing it with wide detours on your subsequent journeys across Yellowstone? If you saw what Bridger saw that day, and if later you were asked to describe what you saw, would you care whether or not the story you ended up telling was perceived as the truth?

Principles of Uncertainty

S he Sings…
…a la rueda, rueda, her voice too soft for the other passengers to hear, yet loud enough to soothe her sweet baby.

She sings, *Dame un besito, y vete para la escuela,* while the subway train whirs along the tracks and the tunnel lights flicker past.

She sings, *Si no quieres ir,* the vibrations of air felt all the way through the quilted denim of the sling pouch, and *Acuéstate a dormir,* before pursing her lips in preparation for planting a delicious kiss—proof that there is no one she loves more in the world than her *chica,* and no one her *chica* loves more than her *mamasita.*

* * *

The Cast:

Maya. Jack. Oskar. Anselm. Ziva. Dorelia. Leon. Alicia. Kathleen Marie. Sally. Audrey. Eduardo. And Angelica, who is sound asleep in her mother's sling pouch, oblivious to the commotion.

Stop Staring!

Course when there's any kind of trouble, who do you think is gonna take the rap? Yo, man, whatchu looking at?

Oskar...

...who was sitting directly across from Maya on the train, set down the magazine and closed his eyes to relieve the strain. He'd been reading an article in exceptionally small print about a new study examining the value of vitamin D supplements. Why, then, he was suddenly remembering standing on the lawn that sloped down from the back porch of his house to the seawall, he couldn't explain. But there you have it: the shimmering sea, the warm wind, the grass a uniform green except for one lone waxy rosette in the center sporting a single dandelion gone to seed.

The Law of Large Numbers

At the same time Anselm, an insurance adjuster for IN-FINICO, was reviewing the morning's calculations, in which he weighed the relevant risks among the sample population against the probable value of investments. Thumbing through his papers, he wasn't entirely confident that his conclusions were correct. In reality, it hardly mattered. The company would set its fees exactly 1.03 percent below the fees of the lowest bid by a competitor, no matter what numbers he presented at the meeting that afternoon.

He looked up, fixing his gaze on the space of the window visible between the young mother with her baby and the large woman to her left. The glass was a transparent black, and the windows of the train on the adjacent track were blurred as the two trains sped by in opposite directions.

He yawned and looked back at his equations, but instead of following the sequence to its end, he attempted to calculate the likelihood of a collision between two subway trains. First, he mentally expanded the sample in order to make the objective risk commensurate with the variance. From there he set out to determine the potential for profitability, weighing the a priori risk against the value of a reasonable premium and wondering, as always, about the outcome.

Ziva Takes Charge.

I was there. I saw the whole thing, and yet my knowledge of the event has been completely disregarded by the authorities, who for some reason have decided that it would have been better if I hadn't been there and have deliberately left me off the list of witnesses, refusing to take my deposition— this despite the fact that, unlike my fellow passengers, I had my eyes wide open and was neither absorbed in a book nor transfixed by a screen. I was, I believe, the only one in the subway car that day who observed the whole extraordinary event start to finish, and I have made it clear that I am prepared to offer a thorough report. Why, then, did the lieutenant at the Ninety-Second Precinct turn me away when I came calling? His excuse was that the case is officially closed. But I can guess what he was thinking. He was thinking that the gray-haired woman dressed in a lime-green woolen suit and the winterfest lace-up shoes she's had reheeled five times could have nothing to tell him that he hadn't already heard.

Sir, I would like to say to him, you should know that looks deceive. You think I am a woman of no account. But my mother's father was a Knight of the Garter. And my father's brother, a lance corporal, was awarded a military medal posthumously after dying of his wounds in Flanders. I had a proper upbringing and to this day will not be caught pushing food onto my spoon with my fingers, or blowing my nose on a serviette. I wait patiently to be served in a shop, and never talk out of turn. And I make sure to introduce myself properly.

Shall we get started then?

Up to…

…the point when the doors closed at approximately 2:47 p.m. and the E train moved on from the Lexington Avenue stop, it still promised to be an ordinary ride on an ordinary day. The passengers in the car were all minding their own business. Even when Leon started belting out his sermon, the ride remained unremarkable by New York standards.

Galatians 5:16

Take a look at yall squandrin yer lives with yer technologic razzle-dazzle, blastin martian men to smithereen and fillin yer ears with smut while the clock is tick-tickin and yall just sittin there not even lustin gainst the Spirit, not carin nuff to lust, yall got yer fancypants phone got yer iPod size of a boiled peanut got whatever it take to keep from pondrin the holy truth.

Now if yall waz led by the Spirit, I say thatted be the end to witchcraft and hairsee and fornification, I say what Jesus say first, that the Spirit is love and joy and peace, and there aint no machine gonna bring yall to the Kingdom. I say there aint no machine gonna light up the way to God.

Rum Cake, Yum.

A la rueda, rueda, de pan y canela, Maya sings, her heart melting with the awareness that all she ever longed for, wished for, prayed for, is contained in the eighteen-pound, seven-ounce bundle in her denim sling. No matter that as soon as her Mr. Cool found out that she was baking a special dessert for him, he was called away on secret business to a place he wasn't allowed to name for an indefinite period. *Hasta nunca,* bye-bye, Veeder's ain. And he just a plumber's assistant, not even licensed. *Mierde cara di niño,* pretending to be a spy to keep from being a father, leaving her not to rot as he expected but to discover true love for the first time in her life. Her little bundle of *chica* love. Nothing else matters now that she has her baby girl. If only the world weren't so dangerous, so full of locos.

You Said It, Girl.

'Cause it ain't uncommon to find yourself surrounded. Anyone on that subway car will know what I'm talking about. First there was the preacher selling heaven like it was pineapples, then the fat lady took to spitting and squealing like she got her toe stuck in the door. Came to me eventually that the lady got laughitis, that was all. She started and she couldn't stop.

What's So Funny?

Lava. Her sister's shriek upon opening up a tub of moldy cream cheese. Rain falling into a pot of boiling water. Also, her little dog Peeweewee—a mix of dachshund and poodle, maybe with a little Chihuahua evident in the ears. Showed up on the stoop one day, she thought he was a water rat. Now he sleeps in her bed.

Boy, is he funny. Pissing on the painted toenails of every caseworker who comes to check on her. Peeweewee, heeheehee.

Consider Yourself Warned.

The problem Leon faced was that the passengers in the fourth car of the E train couldn't have cared less that a man in their midst was ready to steer them forward along the road to salvation. They figured they had better things to think about than their salvation. Even Kathleen Marie, who found everything interesting, kept her eyes fixed on her book, following the example of her daughter, who kept on playing the boring game on her phone only because she was afraid that the man doing the preaching would direct his reproach at her. Even though this was the first time she'd been outside of Iowa, she knew by instinct that the last thing you want when you're visiting New York City is to be singled out.

And then Dorelia, the great-great-granddaughter of a Kanaka Maoli queen, started to chuckle. First she didn't make much noise, just dipped her plump chin against the shelf of her bosom and lifted her pillowy shoulders in jerks. But then the chuckling turned to giggling, and then the giggling turned to flat-out wild laughter that was so loud and odd that Maya stopped whispering her song, Kathleen Marie looked up from her book, and Jack turned off his music because, fuck, what's the use if you can't even hear the bass. Even Leon, who usually was undauntable when it came to preaching, lost track of his place and started preaching about love and joy and peace all over again.

But still the rule held: one mustn't stare in public. Sally nudged her mother to remind her not to stare, Kathleen Marie looked back at her book, and...

Oskar Blinked...
　...registering Dorelia's inappropriate laughter, then closed

his eyes again. Where was he? He'd been remembering running across the lawn in his bare feet, yes, running down the slope, his knees like new burls on two skinny saplings, shorts held up by suspenders, hair shaved so short there were scabs on his scalp.

Who can resist the blowhead of a dandelion?

Watch as he makes his wish, then plumps his cheeks with air—*puff!*—and the seeds scatter in the wind, each borne by its tiny silk parachute. Listen to the flutter of the flag on the pole at the end of the dock. Wince as the gardener boxes him so hard on the head that he falls over.

Uh-Oh.

And then the LED lights began to flicker, disturbing Alicia, who was reading this sentence in the newspaper, "Indeed, Karl Popper built an illuminating philosophy of science on the idea that science progresses precisely by trying as hard as it can to falsify its hypotheses," and Kathleen Marie, who was reading these sentences in the book she'd found at her mother's house after the funeral, "'Oh my God,' Celeste said, smoothing down her skirt as she returned from the bathroom. 'My poor bladder.'" Even Jack, who was playing *Legend of the Cryptids,* and Sally, who was playing *What's the Phrase,* looked up for a moment, but not Audrey, who was about to beat her own best time in *Gods Among Us.* And all the while Ziva—

—Ziva who? We don't have a record of any Ziva.

* * *

The Most Common Causes of Transit Delay:
  Track repair.
  Signal malfunction.
  Dieters who have been weakened by fasting and collapse in a faint.

Times Square
  The E train, in fact, was highly regarded and had one of the best records in the whole New York City transit system for on-time arrival. The cause of the breakdown still hasn't been fully established. MTA officials insist that it had nothing to do with the death of the man who, about the same time, threw himself onto the highly charged third rail in the track bed of the northbound express trains at Times Square.
  The E train was nowhere near Times Square when the man, an apparent suicide, was electrocuted. And really, the brief power outage wouldn't even have earned a mention in the engineer's log if not for the disturbance in the fourth car.

One Was…
  …singing. One was laughing. One was preaching. One was sleeping. Two were reading. Three played video games. The retired late-night announcer for a classical music station based in Astoria was absorbed by a memory from his childhood. One was extracting his pan pipe from its case. Anselm was determining factors that were relevant to a mean

estimate of damages, including the Lexan glass windows, center-facing benches, the fiberglass blind end bonnets, and the dynamic brake propulsion system, with a deceleration rate of 2.5 mph, right when the brakes gave a long, drawn-out squeal, and—

Ziva's Report, Continued

I must confess that I do not ordinarily take the subway. I grew up in a family of some means in the city of Reading in England, and while I no longer have my father's Rolls-Royce at my disposal, I am willing to splurge for a car service run by my entrepreneurial elderly neighbor, Walter, who drives me about for a fraction of what Uber would cost. The reason I did not travel back to Queens in Walter's car on this particular day is this: he did not come to pick me up at the usual time. He wasn't there because there was an accident blocking the Manhattan-bound lanes on the Triborough, and construction work was slowing traffic at the entrance of the Midtown Tunnel, and driving the extra distance to one of the other bridges wasn't worth his prix-fixe fare, though I only learned this later because I have never bothered to get myself a mobile phone and so was unable to receive his message. Even if I had received his message, I still would have taken the subway—which, to my mind, is further evidence that I have no need of a mobile phone. Living on limited resources, I must make careful choices. And though you might say I am splurging on a car service, you can see that when it comes to accessories such as mobile phones and clothes, I am quite frugal.

Excuse me? Why, I'm getting to the point, if you'll be patient!

Yawn.

Heeheehee...

Strife and env'ing and rev'ling...

A dormir, dormir...

Multiplying the mean value times 3.5 to total up the quantifiable damages of the plaintiff, including but not limited to (1) medical bills (emergency services, hospital stays, treatment from specialists, pharmacy expenses, and physical therapy), (2) cost of future medical treatment, (3) lost income, and (4) lost future earning capacity.

The gardener struck him, on behalf of his absent father, who wouldn't have recognized his son in a crowd and came home to preside over the dinner table once a month, on Sundays.

Ding!

Bang!

If, Then

The train ground to a halt with a final jerk. The lights went off. Only the linear points of the dot-matrix route sign stayed on, along with the glow from the various phones.

No one said a word. Leon stopped advocating on behalf of Jesus. Dorelia, who found everything amusing, even managed to turn down the volume of her laughing until it was hardly louder than the effusions of her gaseous digestion. The passengers sat frozen, gripped by suspense. It was as though they'd become aware of the promise of an imminent event that would only occur if they did not move.

The stillness lasted only for an instant that could be measured in a single-digit count of seconds. And then the lights came back on, the air started wheezing through the vents, Dorelia started laughing harder than ever, and it was pretty much back to normal, except that the train remained stalled, which was hardly notable on the New York City transit system.

So What?

Like a train breaking down between Lexington Avenue and Court Square is an event. Yeah, and we sat in the dark for a minute, maybe two. Yeah, and the lights came back on, and we kept sitting there for long enough to give a few weirdos I don't even know their names the chance to go berserk. Yeah, and? I was four hours late to my interview and I still got the job. Like, what's the big deal?

Ziva Proceeds.

But first, allow me to provide some background in the form of a brief account as to how my family, once poor, then rich, became poor again. If I ever do get around to writing my memoir, this chapter would be titled "How Major Dormer's Sweet Delights Goes Bankrupt After Mouse Droppings Are Discovered in Jars of His Chutney." Does this give you an idea of the cause of our downfall? It's true that my father was neither a major nor a Dormer, but that's beside the point. The point is that my father was the victim of a competitor's sabotage. I may have only gossip and innuendo to go on, but I know it, in the same way that I know what happened to that baby on the E train.

I am an unassuming woman, but I know many things. I know you want to hear about the baby. I'll explain about the baby. First, though, I want to go on record to say that someone from a company I am prohibited from naming because of libel laws in my beloved homeland bribed one or more of my father's employees at his Reading plant to stir potentially deadly bacteria into the vats of chutney, thus endangering the lives of thousands but killing only one poor soul, a grandmother in Liverpool, and driving my father out of—

Jack, Audrey, and Sally…
…resumed playing their video games. Alicia and Kathleen Marie continued to read. Dorelia raised the volume of her laughter. Anselm and Oskar were lost in thought again. Maya sang in whispers to Angelica. Leon licked his lips and smiled weakly. Eduardo put his pan pipe to his lips, then paused as he caught sight of Maya's lips forming a scream he couldn't hear.

Dios mio!
What's going on?

I don't know.
Angelica!
Call 911!
I can't get service!
Pull the emergency brake!
But we're not moving!
Why is that woman screaming?
Why is that woman laughing?
Call the driver. Use the intercom. Tell him—
What?

Unum

It was sick, like it was all a setup. I thought it was one of those candid-camera things to see how stupid we were. There was the Cuban girl screaming that she lost her baby. But she didn't lose her baby. A baby can't just go and get lost when you're all stuck on a subway car underneath the East River. It was probably just curled up at the bottom of the sack. And the whole time, there's that fat lady laughing out loud. Come on, man, think about it. It didn't happen because it couldn't happen. I knew it all along. That's why I didn't do nothing. Then I'm the one gets booked. What does that say about our goddamn *e pluribus u—*

Ziva Interrupts.

It says everybody is used to easy answers speedily delivered. And so I will not linger on the details of my background, I will move on past my aborted education at the University of

London to my unhappy year as a secretary for a predatory chartered accountant who routinely patted my backside to reassure himself that it was still there, through the deaths of my parents and a series of jobs that never worked out but kept me too busy to think about marriage, to New York, 1979, where my older sister was living with her three daughters, after having recently divorced her American husband. The said husband turned out to be living a secret life under a different name, with a second wife and two children, but that's another matter, irrelevant to the subject at hand. I need only say that with the husband gone, I helped my sister raise her girls. Shortly after my sister died in 1985, my savings ran out, so I went out looking for a job and found one as a nanny for a family on Central Park West.

I moved to my current apartment in Forest Hills, the years passed, the children in my charge grew up, I found another family to work for on East Sixty-Seventh Street, I grew old, I spent my hard-earned money on Walter's car service, sparing myself from the long climb down to the subway and back up again, but because Walter was stuck in traffic for two hours and ended up turning around and heading back to Queens, I had to take the subway home from work on that fateful day.

The Day the E Train Stalled and a Baby Disappeared into Thin Air
Just like that.
The poor mother.

And to think of that obese woman laughing the whole while.

And the preacher holding on to the pole, looking utterly baffled.

And Kathleen Marie panicking, convinced that there was a terrorist among the group, while her daughter gave up trying not to stare and stared at Maya, who was still screaming, and at Dorelia beside her, who was still laughing.

While Audrey and Alicia and Anselm scrambled to help.

And Oskar watched sleepily, as if from a great distance.

And Jack remained in his corner seat, avoiding any involvement because he already knew that whatever happened, he'd be blamed.

The Investigation

It would have been hard not to perceive that the sling pouch was empty. But in the aftermath, only Sally would confirm Maya's claim that the baby was truly gone, and no one believed her. Audrey and Alicia would be persuaded by Anselm, who attributed the mother's confusion to the train's temporary power outage. Oskar would say he'd been dozing and wasn't sure what happened. Kathleen Marie would accuse Jack of causing a distraction in order to prepare for the attack he was plotting. Jack would plead innocence. Dorelia would be identified as a schizophrenic who had stopped taking medication she couldn't afford. The investigating agents gave up on Eduardo the pan-pipe player, who was deaf and couldn't sign in English. As for Ziva—

none of the other passengers would confirm that Ziva had been present.

I Was There.

And though my calls to the police go unanswered, I will not be silent. It should be worth something that I remember the faces of all participants and am able to identify the impostors who have multiplied exponentially, as interest in the story has spread. Judging from the number of people who swear that they saw it, you'd think there must have been a crowd of thousands stuffed into that subway car. In fact, there were only eleven passengers. Plus yours truly—the unremarkable Ziva—makes twelve altogether. Oh, and the baby. I will tell you what happened to that baby, but first—

The Child Herself

Why, she wasn't even a year old. Of course she couldn't describe what happened to her in that gap between the moment after the sling pouch Maya was carrying suddenly went slack, like a deflated balloon, and when it filled again, an interval lasting hardly more than a minute, two minutes at the most, though it was long enough for several passengers to spring from the benches in panic, bellowing, bumping into each other, some diving for the subway intercom, others falling to their knees and searching under the benches, behind shopping bags and briefcases, all of them temporarily convinced that the baby had indeed gone missing. Especially after the purple Binky the baby had been sucking was found on the bench between Dorelia and Maya.

Some had suspicions they wouldn't admit to later: that Leon had grabbed the baby when the lights went dark and thrown it out the window, or Jack had stolen the baby and stuffed it in his backpack, or Dorelia had eaten it.

And then Angelica came back. Sally was the one who noticed first, just as the train started moving forward again with a jerk, throwing the passengers off balance, so that they stumbled into each other before reaching for the poles and overhead handles.

Why, there she is. She must have been there all along! Wriggling in the pouch, bending her neck back to gaze serenely at the faces of startled strangers. There she is, indeed. Angelica, you naughty girl, where were you hiding?

From Dorelia's Perspective
She had never, ever seen anything funnier!

By the Time…
…Angelica was five, she'd heard her mother tell the story more times than she could count, so many times that she wasn't sure if she actually remembered the incident, or if she'd made up the faint memory in an effort to complement the few verifiable facts. Did she imagine falling through a darkness so absolute that she wasn't sure if she was plunging down into a bottomless hole or shooting up through the universe? Was it her own hysteria she felt at the loss that even

her baby brain could perceive, or the hysteria her mother described in her retelling? Had she really tumbled head over heels from the visible world into another dimension?

She remembers, or remembers imagining, that as she fell she heard the sound of laughter in the distance. Later she would compare it to the piping of birds across the park. What a sweet sound. She was desperate to hear it more clearly. She wanted to be moving toward the laughter, not away from it, so she began to resist what seemed inevitable. She clawed against the emptiness, dragging her baby nails against the sides of the abyss in an effort to stop her plunge. And to her amazement, she managed to slow the speed of her fall until she felt as if she were merely sinking, as if into saltwater. She gave a fierce kick and was suspended, then cupped the emptiness in her hands and pulled herself up toward the surface of her life, swimming back to where the laughter was coming from, back to her nest in the denim sling pouch strung across her mother's chest.

Everybody was staring at her. Everybody would always stare at her. Even if they weren't staring with their eyes, they were staring in their thoughts. She may have looked perfectly normal with her dark pigtails and big round eyes. But when she came back after disappearing on the E train underneath the East River, she was different. She couldn't help it.

Early on, she listened to the story with fascination. But as the story evolved and Maya began to embellish it with details about Dorelia and Leon and Anselm and the others, listeners began to laugh. This was not the same sweet laughter Angelica had heard while she was falling. This was sour laughter, curdled like old milk, and she took to hiding beneath the table whenever her mother launched into a new retelling.

It wasn't until she'd started school and learned to read that she felt curious about how the experience would affect her in the years to come. That's when she began to look toward the future with great anticipation.

Report of a Disturbance

It turned out that an MTA employee riding in Car Five had watched the ruckus through the window panel of the door, and he put in a call to the transit police over his walkie-talkie. Two policemen were already waiting at Court Square when the train arrived, and more showed up within minutes. The passengers from Car Four were instructed to assemble on the south end of the platform, and they were interviewed one by one.

According to the official report, there was not sufficient evidence that a kidnapping had occurred, or had even been attempted. They couldn't even ascertain whether the baby had gone missing at all. Maybe the mother had been mistaken. And yet her testimony was echoed by the girl from Iowa. And there were others suggesting that Homeland Security should be brought in. Passersby lingered, drawn by the sight of the extra police. As rumors spread, people from the street came down to see what they'd missed. They wanted to know what had happened, and if there were casualties, and who was responsible. They wanted to see what the police would do to prove their mettle.

#freakoutontheetrain

Kathleen Marie and Sally continued on to Sutphin Boulevard. Anselm arrived on time at his next meeting. Leon and Eduardo boarded different cars of a westbound train and headed back into Manhattan. Maya and Angelica went to visit a cousin. Jack was handcuffed and charged with disturbing the peace. Audrey went to one coffee shop, Alicia to another, and both unwittingly used the same hashtag for their tweets. Ziva lingered at the Court Square station, hoping to find someone who would listen to her.

Only Oskar…

…went directly home. He transferred to the bus and arrived on his block shortly before 3:30 that afternoon. He let himself into the brownstone and walked slowly up the two flights of creaking stairs to his apartment. Fiddling with the key in the sticky deadbolt, which needed a delicate touch, he had a realization. That time when he was a small boy and his father's gardener hit him for blowing dandelion seeds across the lawn, it had hurt. But here's the thing: he had managed to live for another sixty years without ever getting hurt again. All this time, he hadn't really noticed how very careful he'd been, how deliberately he'd stuck to his routines in an effort to keep himself safe.

Unlike the Victim of the Electrocution in Times Square

According to the local evening news, some straphangers rushed to the ledge to help him and backed off when they saw sparks. That was the story that filled out the evening news that night—not the story of the E train, which no channel bothered to cover because no one would have believed it.

All Is Happiness, All Is Good.

The story, Maya liked to say, always ended with Eduardo. It was Eduardo the pan-pipe player, she said, who brought everything under control. Once the train had started moving again and Angelica was nestled safely in the sling pouch, Eduardo took it upon himself to entertain the passengers with the melancholy tune of a *yaravi,* which he couldn't hear, of course, but which had the intended effect of providing a soothing focus of attention, drawing everyone away from the confusion of the moment to the southern sierra of Peru. Leon sat down, Dorelia stopped laughing, Angelica fell asleep. It was so sweet, Maya would say. Eduardo played as if stirring time with a spoon. He mixed and mixed, adding a little pinch of this and a little of that to blend the notes together. Until the train reached Court Square and the passengers headed to their next destination, all except Jack, there was nada to worry about, Maya would have liked to say. Her *chica* had come back.

The only detail Maya never knew was that charges against Jack were eventually dropped, thanks to Oskar, who returned to the Court Square precinct later that afternoon to point out that Jack couldn't be guilty if none of this had ever happened.

The Silver Pearl

The microfilm showed a water stain on the marbled cover, its tentacles extending toward the embossed lettering of the title. The filigreed etching on the frontispiece included a dedication to an earl from his "most obedient servant." I don't recall the author's name, or the name of the earl. I scrolled through the reel so long ago that I've forgotten important details. I do remember that an early reader had penned some heated remarks in the margins of the prologue.

It was an odd prologue, to be sure, beginning with a long rant about the general uselessness of art, provoking from the anonymous reader comments that included "Vaporous flummery!" and "Piffle!" In one passage, over which the reader had scrawled a large X, the author argued forcefully that art has no measurable benefits, art begets only more art, art leads away from truth and offers no antidotes to the world's problems. The author denounced painting, music, sculpture, and theater before singling out literature, comparing it to the marks left on skin when a mosquito bite is scratched. Concerning education, the author maintained that there are only two subjects worth studying: history, which can teach humanity to avoid repeating stupid mistakes, and "gloriously useful science."

It became clear that the author regarded science not in its broadest, most traditional sense, as any form of knowledge that distinguishes itself from ignorance. Rather, he (she?) was championing only *natural* science, with its concern for the physical world, its quantifiable results, its classification of facts, and, most important, its predictive powers. The author went on at length about this last quality. I remember that next to the passage, the reader had written a long note that was impossible to decipher no matter how much I turned up the magnification on the machine. This seemed to be the point where the reader stopped reading, for there was no more commentary on the pages that followed.

* * *

Turning from the prologue to the first chapter, I was surprised, given the author's disdain for literature, to find all the trappings of a novel. The chapter opened with a long description of a young girl named Williamina, pale and dark-eyed, wandering along the banks of the River Tay on the outskirts of the city of Dundee. She was dressed in a simple yellow frock, with a lace bonnet tied tightly over her coils of braids. What stood out most to me was that she wore no shoes. I'm not sure if I'm remembering correctly that she squished her bare toes in the mud—perhaps *squished* is my word—but I'm sure I'm right in recalling that she was prying freshwater mussels from the sides of rocks in the shallows.

Her fingers started to tingle from the cold water, and as she paused in her task to warm her hands in her pockets, the chatter of schoolgirls caught her attention. She watched them hurry along the path. One of the girls waved to her. She waved back. There had been a time when she longed to be among them, to finish her education and learn everything there was to know. She had given up school after her mother died. Now the students seemed as far from reach as a procession of clergy in church, and Williamina could only gaze at them with distant reverence.

She resumed her search for mussels. Soon she had filled her basket, and she returned to the cottage where she lived with her father. He was a widower who worked as a gilder, and evidence of his trade was apparent in the clutter of gilded picture frames and furniture. Though renowned for his skill, the father produced his goods faster than he could sell them, and he stuffed the cottage with the overflow and then scolded his daughter for failing to keep the rooms dusted and orderly.

The housework could wait, for Williamina had a more

important task. She dumped her harvest of mussels onto the table. The clattering reminded her of the sound the waves made along the pebbly edge of the firth. She spread them out and then attacked them with a knife, prying them open one by one. I remember mistakenly thinking as I was reading that the girl was preparing dinner. Instead, I soon learned that she was searching for a delicate gem found only in the freshwater mussels of that region, a type of small pearl, usually no more than a quarter inch across, with a lustrous silver hue.

A sweat broke out on her forehead as she continued with her concentrated work. It looked like her most recent harvest was going to disappoint her. Only when she had pried open the very last mussel and scooped out the flesh was her effort rewarded. Attached to the shell was the biggest pearl she'd ever found, silver and perfectly round and as big as an acorn!

She added the treasure to her collection of pearls, dropping it into a special jar. This jar, the author took the time to explain, had been intended as a powder jar and was made of frosted glass, painted with pink roses, and crowned with a gilded lid. After the gilder had dropped the jar on the floor and chipped the glass, no one would purchase it, so he had given it to his daughter. The jar was the one gift Williamina had ever received from her father, and she cherished it. It was a beautiful vessel, and now that it was filled with pearls, the chip in the glass was hardly noticeable.

* * *

Williamina loved her father, but in reality he was a mercenary man who cared for nothing but making a profit. When he heard about a certain eel-faced accountant who was in search of a wife to accompany him to America, Williamina's father acted quickly. He betrothed his daughter to the eel, or, in terms the eel preferred, given his accounting expertise, the father traded the family asset at fair market value.

And so poor Williamina, sold for five hundred guineas, found herself at sea, en route from Liverpool to Boston in a second-class berth, her slender, finless husband squirming on top of her, his slick back cold to her touch, his energetic sperm wiggling in a pack in pursuit of their prey. She was pregnant by the time she arrived in New England. She dismissed the first episodes of nausea as the lingering effects of seasickness and set about arranging the small furnished flat they'd rented on Greenough Lane, washing the dusty dishes and sweeping up the rat droppings, while her husband went to work as an accountant for a dry goods warehouse.

The eel kept sloppy ledgers, and it only took three months for him to be fired from his job. Williamina, who by then understood the significance of her swelling belly, took out the jar she'd kept hidden in her trunk and sold some of her precious pearls to pay for a rocking bassinette. A daughter with a fine mop of black hair and eyes as dark as her mother's was born on the seventh of June. The eel reportedly shrank from the sight of the infant. His repulsion was never fully explained, though I suppose the author was implying that the eel felt ashamed at being unable to provide for his family. After a year in Boston, he failed to find new employment. Being an eel, he took advantage of his ability to swim backward and returned across the ocean to Scotland, leaving his wife and child to fend for themselves.

In her husband's absence, Williamina sold her pearls by the handful to pay the landlord and the grocer. She spent her last and largest pearl, the one as big as an acorn, on a bed for her daughter, who had outgrown the bassinette. After the jar was empty, Williamina went out looking for work. Leaving her daughter in the care of a neighbor, she responded to an advertisement for a seamstress, but after a week's trial she was dismissed for being too slow with her hemming. She spent many hard months taking in washing and selling flowers on the street.

One day she struck up a conversation with a gentleman who had purchased flowers from her. I remember that he carried a closed umbrella, and his cheeks stuck out like mahogany doorknobs above his whiskers. He revealed that the flowers were for his wife, who was out of sorts because their beloved old servant had gone to live with her daughter in Albany. The gentleman asked Williamina if she knew of any girls who were looking for domestic employment. She said she did know of just the right girl, and she agreed to send her to the gentleman's house in Cambridge. Williamina herself arrived at the address the next day.

Upon opening the door, the gentleman had a good chuckle

as he realized that the flower girl had recommended herself. He hired Williamina on the spot.

* * *

The gentleman, Williamina learned, was a professor at Harvard. In the weeks that followed, she was surprised to find that the professor showed little interest in the books in his study. He stayed out most every night and slept away the mornings. His wife appeared oblivious to her husband's dissolute ways. Williamina felt some pity for her, but she was grateful to have steady work and happily accepted when the professor's wife invited Williamina and her daughter to take up residence in the cozy suite on the third floor.

She enjoyed the peacefulness of her routines and never complained. She dusted and washed and swept and cooked, always keeping one eye on her little daughter, who followed her around the house. She told herself that someday her daughter would go to school, and, unlike her mother, she would complete her education, learning everything there was to know.

If Williamina felt any displeasure in her work, it was in her opinion of the professor. She believed a Harvard professor had a responsibility to be a model of decency for his students. It pained her to hear the front door creak open when he returned home in the morning. She told herself that the professor's nightly philandering was none of her business, but one day his eyes seemed more bloodshot than usual, and she felt she had to speak out.

"As my father used to say, sir," she murmured, pouring him his morning tea at noon, "God made darkness to keep us home at night."

Her suspicions became clear to the professor, and he set out to defend his innocence in a manner that took Williamina by surprise. He insisted that he had done no wrong and she had judged him unfairly. He even went so far as to invite Williamina to accompany him when he went out the following night. Her first impulse was to take offense, thinking he meant her to indulge with him in unspeakable iniquities. But the professor was so insistent in his urging and so persuasive in his claim of innocence that she couldn't contain her curiosity. She accepted his invitation.

* * *

The professor's wife was cheerful when her maid and her husband left the house together the next evening after dinner. She even promised to read to Williamina's daughter and tuck her into bed. I remember worrying on Williamina's behalf. Surely the professor was up to no good, and his wife was in on the conspiracy. My imagination raced ahead of the story as I scrolled through the microfilm. I feared most for Williamina's daughter, left in the care of the professor's wife. I couldn't stand waiting to find out what was going to happen, and I remember skipping over several pages in a panic.

What the author finally revealed, after teasing me with unhappy possibilities, was that Williamina's employer was a professor of astronomy. He led his servant not to an opium den or brothel but, rather, to the College Observatory on Concord Avenue. They climbed the wooden stairs into the dome, where the professor's students were already busily at work taking turns peering up at the night sky and recording their astronomical observations.

The professor met his charges with a gruff hello. Without introducing his visitor, he gestured to the student at the telescope, who surrendered his place to Williamina. The professor explained to her how to look through the eyepiece and adjust the focus. Soon she was gazing deep into the milky heavens.

She remembered with some sadness the daydreams she used to indulge in as a young girl. She would have liked to devote her life to the study of the galaxy, or the sea, or the human body, or history, or language, or anything at all, as long as she never stopped learning. She thought she heard murmurs and laughter coming from behind her. Looking up at the distant stars, she did not confess to the male students that she would rather have spent her nights trying to solve the mysteries of the universe than her days washing the undergarments of her employers. Nor did she give the professor what he wanted and offer exclamations of awe. She did not compare the view through the telescope to a display in a jeweler's window. She did not even say that she was very grateful to be given the opportunity to visit the Observatory.

Instead, adjusting the knob to sharpen the focus of the powerful telescope, she said, "It's not just light I see. There's plenty of dust up in the sky!"

The students laughed heartily at that—of course a maid would see dust—and one of them cried out, "Give the old girl a broom!"

The telescope was trained on the constellation of Orion. The author explained that the professor was trying to account for a new cosmic element that was green when viewed with the naked eye but sometimes showed up as a darker shadow when photographed through the optical tube. He wanted to prove the existence of nebulae in the constellation but so far had failed to produce consistent evidence.

A maid who could see dust in the sky was a vast improvement over the professor's students, who claimed to see nothing of interest. That alone raised the professor's estimation of her intellectual abilities. After her turn at the telescope, she said nothing more, but the professor was conscious of the intensity of her attention as she watched from the periphery of the room. On his way home, he asked her if she would mind helping him with his research. She said she wouldn't mind at all.

In the months that followed, he brought home glass plates for Williamina to examine in her spare time. She studied them at length. Each plate presented to her a complicated blend of light and shadow, with hidden shapes that she could always find if she looked hard enough. The professor taught her how to identify what he called, if I remember correctly, the "spectral emissions of visible hydrogen." To keep track of her observations, she developed a notation system that the professor adopted for his research. He was delighted with her work, and he was quick to agree when, after her daughter began attending school the following September, Williamina gingerly suggested that she might be more helpful to the professor in his laboratory than in his home.

* * *

The microfilm containing this book had been part of a collection that was discarded by my library and subsequently destroyed. I haven't had any luck finding another copy. I have since verified, however, that Williamina Fleming was a real person. You can look her up yourself and find out the basics of her life—that she was born in Scotland, immigrated to America, was abandoned by her husband and later employed as a maid, went to work in a Harvard laboratory, and, in a photograph captured through a telescope, discovered a nebula in the shape of a horse's head. Her contribution to science accounted for the author's interest in her, I assume. But the basics won't tell you much about Williamina. The book included extensive information I haven't been able to verify, including the following story from the final chapter:

Williamina, by then the mother of a college graduate and grandmother of a young boy, was walking along the beach near the seaside cottage where she had settled in her retirement. Her grandson walked beside her. She carried a bucket to hold whatever her grandson chose to collect. Of the many things that ended up in the bucket, there was, I remember, a fragment of yellow quartz, a dried starfish, a piece of bleached driftwood, and an unusual shell that had the length of a razor clam, the concentric ridges of a feathered oyster, and iridescent spots.

They carried the bucket home and examined the contents one by one. Williamina held the quartz up to the window to show her grandson the veins when the light shone through it. She pointed out the suction cups on the legs of the starfish. She set the driftwood on the windowsill. And then, at last, Williamina reached for the seashell.

I paused before scrolling to the final page. It occurred to me, with the conclusion imminent, that I wasn't sure whether Williamina was happy with the life she'd led. The author had not been as forthcoming on that score as I would have wished. And then, in this interval, I realized that I already knew what I was about to read. There was no guessing involved. I cannot forecast the punch line of the most obvious joke or even tell you what I am going to have for dinner tonight, but before I finished the book, I knew how it would end, as if I'd written it myself. I knew that Williamina would wiggle a knife into the hinge of the shell, forcing it open. I foresaw that after digging away the meat she would find a silver pearl as big as an acorn! I was even right about the exclamation mark. But I was left feeling satisfied, and, upon reflection, somewhat puzzled. Had the author not realized that by giving his readers the opportunity to see into the future, he had introduced the possibility that the predictions of natural science are rivaled by the prophecies of art?

The Maverick

Our differences were obvious. He was thin. I, on the other hand, have been known to break the scale. He was ambitious, fixed on the prize. I tend to be lazy, lumbering, and easily distracted. He insisted on ordering prime rib for dinner, even when we couldn't afford it. I adapt easily to adverse conditions and enjoy equally a handful of mashed ants sweetened with sap, a bag of shrimp shells scavenged from the Dumpster, or a grasshopper, wings and legs removed. He liked fancy hotels. I can sleep soundly on a bed of aromatic pine needles or on a feather mattress in a suburban home while the occupants are out of town—it's all the same to me. He could be charming whenever the situation called for it. I like to blend in with the crowd and have learned to transform myself with the simplest disguises. I keep a cache of various hats and sunglasses for just this purpose. He craved fanfare. I prefer anonymity. I can, when necessary, disappear in the blink of an eye. He was an expert at self-promotion. I am an expert at observation. He was young. I was already old when we first met. He was trained as a mule-spinner in a textile mill. I was trained to survive. He was good at checkers. I am good at riddles. For example, I can identify what goes up and never comes down. And I can show you something you'll see less of as it grows.

Of course, it goes without saying that I know about bears. I know more about bears than you'd ever want to hear. I've been around town, as they say. I am very fat and very old. I never expected to be so old. I've lived so long that there are no surprises left. The stories I could tell. Really, though, he was the true storyteller. I have always preferred to listen. And as soon as I'm done answering your question, I'll shut up.

It was long ago, long before your grandparents were born, when a ticket to see a dancing bear cost a mere two cents. I listened to him while he emptied a bottle of brandy and talked about the peculiar sport of jumping waterfalls. But it wasn't a sport to him. It was an art he'd perfected as a boy jumping from the bridge in Pawtucket. The fact that he remained impoverished and unrecognized only made him more certain that he was deserving. He had courage. He had vision. Most important, he had a surefire technique, the details of which he guarded jealously. But the more he drank, the more freely he talked. I kept listening. He must have assumed I couldn't understand. He was a man who wanted to be a hero. I was just a bear, already stiffening with age and growing ever stouter.

Wear a snug-fitting shirt, he said, and loose pants of white cotton. Breathe in when you leap. Pin your arms against your sides. Bend your knees then snap your legs straight just before you hit the water. Let the current carry you away. Find a rock to hold on to downriver. Only when the audience has concluded that you've been swept to a watery grave should you burst up through the surface and wave to them.

Oh, and whenever you jump, make sure you're good and drunk. That's essential. Be a better friend to the bottle than the bottle is to you.

He jumped Passaic Falls when he was twenty-seven. He jumped from the top of a ship's mast into the Hudson River when he was twenty-eight. A few weeks later he jumped Paterson Falls. Finally, on a rainy October afternoon, when he was twenty-nine, he jumped eighty feet over Niagara Falls. That made him famous, for certain. But he wasn't famous enough by his own measure. He could never be famous enough.

We met in Buffalo. He was wearing a sailor's jacket. I was dancing on a stage at McCleary's Museum. He bought me for ten dollars and led me away on a leash. We sat in a bar. He talked for hours, as if he'd never before met anyone willing to listen to him. I listened while he told me about his impossible dream of success. His next jump, he said, would be more daring than the last. He vowed to jump Niagara Falls from a platform 120 feet high. He told me not to warn him against it. He'd made up his mind. I could see he was a stubborn fool, but I also admired him more than I care to admit. He was the first individual I'd ever met who was truly fearless.

He jumped for the second time into Niagara Falls on October 17. I sat among an audience of ladies who had paid a fee to watch from a boat. He entered the water with one knee bent. The ladies in the boat exclaimed at the splash, and those closest to me buried their trembling fingers in my fur. We all thought he was dead. And then he popped from the water, waved to us, and swam on his back to shore.

There are many routes to fame, but the quickest and surest is the one I traversed with my friend, there and back. It's true that almost no one remembers me anymore. I've lived too long. But I once became very famous very quickly. You could do it, too. Let me suggest, however, that jumping from a high platform into the falls wearing a snug-fitting shirt and white trousers, with your arms tight against your sides, won't be enough. Nothing is enough unless you advertise.

With each successive jump, he became savvier about publicity. He began printing out announcements headed with his motto: "Some things can be done as well as others"— whatever that meant, I never quite understood. He paid boys to put up the flyers around town, in stores and music halls and taverns. The point was to convince every segment of the public that there was no better way to spend their time than watching a man risk his life for the sheer thrill of it.

They called him doggone crazy back home in Pawtucket.

They called him spectacular in Hoboken. They called him astonishing in Niagara. But he wanted more than passing notice. He wanted to have a permanent place in history.

He decided that he hadn't paid enough attention to his appearance. He spent his earnings on a manicurist and a shave at the barber. He added a black silk scarf to his wardrobe. He bought himself a pair of gold cufflinks. I could have told him to leave his cufflinks at home. Baubles such as cufflinks are like berries to young bears—the more one has, the more one wants. A few won't satisfy. I should know.

It's true that I haven't stripped a bush of berries in a long time. But I'd rather resist temptation than have to suffer when there's nothing left. I won't let myself get started. I don't waste my time remembering that blueberries were once my favorite, or that tender wintergreen can be found growing beneath pine trees. Isn't it better to learn to take pleasure in what is most readily available?

Anyway, you didn't seek me out to talk about berries. You want to know about the man who was famous, but not famous enough, for jumping from high platforms into the raging tumult of cascading rivers. He had fine gold cufflinks, a silk scarf, a snug-fitting shirt, and white trousers. Add a tried-and-true technique and several fortifying snifters of brandy, and it still wasn't enough.

What was missing? he wondered aloud. We were at an establishment called The Recess, just the two of us. He was scheduled to jump the local falls the next day. He was told to expect a crowd of hundreds. But he wanted a crowd of thousands. How could he make the world stop turning and pay attention to him?

I yawned. He watched me yawn. There you have it. It was late at night, I couldn't help but yawn. He looked into my yawning mouth and saw his future. He saw renown, wealth, adulation beyond anything he'd yet experienced. He followed my wide pink tongue into the black chasm and saw his own potential.

The next day, a fine, bright Indian summer day, he invited me to accompany him up to the platform that had been erected above the falls. After delivering his usual speech, in which he compared himself favorably to Alexander the Great, Napoleon, and God, he jumped. Though he was still enjoying the effects of the previous night's brandy, his form was perfect: arms tight against his sides, knees bent then snapping straight so he entered the water with hardly a sound. The audience waited with increasing fear for him to emerge. He didn't emerge for several minutes. Nervous murmurs rippled through the crowd. And then there he was, bobbing along the river, smiling and waving. The audience cheered.

Their cheers weren't enough for a man who was born to feel unappreciated. So this is what he did to invite them to cheer louder: he climbed out of the river, up the stone steps to the top of the gorge, and up the ladder to the platform where I was waiting. I noticed that his cufflinks were gone. He smiled at me, a strange, indecent smile that made me wonder if he longed for more than fame. And then he shoved me. That's right—he jammed an elbow deep into my fat belly and pushed. I wasn't prepared for the assault, and with a roar of outrage I fell backward, off the platform.

As the local newspaper reported, I made several promiscuous turns in midair, and then struck the water stern first.

What my famous friend discovered was that if you want to succeed, don't try to do it alone. Any challenge is less agreeable when you confront it alone. Find someone you can trust, a loyal, brave collaborator.

He trusted me. I listened to his stories, his complaints, his secret dreams. And in fact I'd trusted him. When he led me away from Jonathan McCleary's Buffalo Museum, he saved me from the humiliation of dancing in public. He wanted me near him. I hadn't been wanted like that since my mother banished me from the den. I was his friend, and he was mine. We were a swell pair, we complemented each other. He liked to talk; I liked to listen. I was content to keep him company—until the day he pushed me from the platform over the Genesee Falls.

I made a big splash, you might say. The audience loved me. Word got out that the show was going to be repeated. Tempting fate, he scheduled the next jump for Friday the thirteenth.

Unlucky Friday, day of scripted doom. He knew what he was doing. He would suffer. He would be buried. And then, hah, he would rise again, dripping wet and as smug as ever. He would climb out of the river and up the ladder. And then, in front of his biggest audience ever, he would humiliate an old, fat bear by pushing him off the platform.

Unless I pushed him first.

I was trained to survive. I have learned not to be particular. I am as readily satisfied with rotten apples as I am with a hunk of corned beef. The only thing I don't like is to be the center of attention. Survivors will go to great lengths to avoid being the center of attention.

I wanted to be overlooked. He wanted to be noticed. There was no greater difference than this between us. Our friendship was testament to the cliché that opposites attract. He trusted me. I wish he could have gone on trusting me to the end. But in the moment after I discreetly bumped him with my hindquarters, knocking him off the platform, he realized that I wasn't a true friend. He had no true friends. He was alone, falling through the air into the river. It was necessary for him to be alone.

Instead of falling straight down on this, his final jump, he fell cockeyed. He must have realized what was happening in the split second before it was over. He knew what I'd done to him. He hit the water with a resounding smack. And, at last, he became truly famous.

The audience refused to believe he died that day. People speculated that he hid in a cave behind the falls until the anxious crowd dispersed. In the months that followed, rumors spread, and my friend was the subject of sightings around the world: he was seen boarding a trolley in San Francisco, riding a bicycle through New York's Central Park, and flying a kite on a beach on the Italian island of Sardinia. The reports continued even after his body was found downriver in the shallows the following spring. He was more famous than he had ever hoped to become, thanks to me.

I am sorry for it. I am sorry not because I caused him to suffer but because I let him trick me into helping him achieve his dream. I thought I was saving myself by shoving him before he could shove me, but in that instant when he was tipping backward off the platform, I looked over my shoulder at him, our eyes met, and I saw a flash of something approaching satisfaction.

I earned my keep by giving him the kind of fame that would outlast his lifetime. I turned him into a survivor—the only kind of survivor he ever wanted to be. He finally became a legend on that day, while I was destined to be forgotten. There's no room in his story for an old dancing bear. I was left to climb unnoticed down the platform and slip back into the crowd, taking refuge again in anonymity, condemned to survive in my own way and grow ever older, more haggard, hungrier, lonelier, after having succeeded in losing the only friend I ever had.

Teardrop

He came to the door wearing Bermuda shorts and a Jockey undershirt, gripping a ribbed tumbler I assumed was full of water. Only after he stumbled over the weather strip and I accepted his damp hand to shake did I put two and two together: the liquid in his glass was his beloved Smirnoff, poured from a bottle I knew he kept in the freezer because I had seen him reach for it at parties when he was mixing up a round of screwdrivers.

We were all drinkers in our extended family, but my brother-in-law had emerged over the past year as the only full-fledged drunk among us. I congratulated myself on foreseeing his decline. I had always thought he was a loser.

I did not say aloud, *My sister had a dozen better men*

vying for her love, and she made the mistake of choosing you.
Instead, I asked him, "How are you?"

"Hanging in there," he said, pulling his hand from my grip
and covering his mouth in a failed attempt to muffle himself
as he cleared his throat.

As I stood there awkwardly, waiting for him to invite
me inside, his vaguely wearied expression suddenly lit with
interest. I turned to see what he was looking at just as
Bob, the family cat, crept from behind the trunk of an old
hemlock in the front yard, stalking an invisible prey in the
pine needles.

"Is Jody ready?"

My question stirred my brother-in-law to action. "Jo!" he
howled into the house. "Jo, your aunt is here!"

I heard a distant thud, and Jody's voice yelling in reply.
"Be there in a sec!"

"What do you hear from Ellie?" I asked. Ellie, my sister,
was in the hospital, recovering from a double mastectomy.

"She's coming home tomorrow morning," he said, which
I already knew, since I had visited her the previous day, and
every day before that. Today was the only day I would not
visit my sister in the hospital, for I had agreed to her request
to concentrate on her daughter, who might need, my sister
suggested, a little extra attention.

"I would pick Sis up myself, but I have to go into the office
early," I said, while with my eyes I reminded my brother-
in-law that he was a lazy pig who had lost his job back
in December and had settled contentedly into dependence

upon his wife, an overworked high school social studies teacher. And now that my sister had cancer, my brother-in-law could think of nothing else to do but fill his glass with booze.

"No problem, we're all set. Whoa there!" He staggered, causing his morning aperitif to slosh over the rim, as Jody, dressed in a polka-dot T-shirt and denim overalls with grass stains on both knees, squeezed between her father and the doorway and leaped into my arms.

"My little lady!"

"My bestest auntie!"

"I'm your only auntie." I spit on my fingers and rubbed the dirt smudge off her cheek.

"And you're my bestest papa!" she said, leaning out of my arms in an appeal toward her father, grabbing him by his unkempt goatee and pulling his face close in order to cover it with kisses.

"You're my bestest girl!" her father chimed, beaming, reeking of that particular spirit he preferred because of his idiotic belief that it couldn't be detected by a Breathalyzer. "Now you be good today, no shenanigans, eh."

"I'll have her home by—" I began as Jody wriggled out of my arms. She landed on her bottom before I could catch her.

"Ow!"

"Oh, baby, are you okay?"

Her assurance that she was just fine took the form of crazy giggles and a manic lunge for the cat, which she caught up in her arms and squeezed so hard that any other cat would have scratched in fury, while Bob just settled into the embrace with a loud rattle of a purr.

"Take care of Papa," Jody ordered Bob. As she lowered him to the ground headfirst, the cat righted himself with a maneuver that looked very much like a backflip.

"Love you," called her father as I took Jody's hand and led her to the car.

"Love you back!" Jody shouted, for all the neighborhood to hear.

The year was 1965. Lucky Debonair had just won the Derby and an earthquake had rattled Seattle.

"Did you hear about the earthquake in Seattle?" I asked Jody, turning the page of the newspaper to follow the story.

"Is everyone okay?"

"Yes," I lied, deciding at the last minute that my little niece was not ready for a tale of death and destruction.

"That's good." She put the finishing touches on the smiley face she had been tracing in the dust on the train window. "What are we going to do today?" she asked, forgetting the plans we had made over the phone the previous evening.

"Don't you want to go to the zoo?"

"Yeah," she said, then added, upon consideration, "No."

As the train pulled out of the station, we were joined by two new passengers, who ignored the other empty seats in the car and chose the bench across from us, forcing me to change my position and point my knees at an uncomfortable diagonal. The woman was pale, with gray hair and fuzzy eyebrows the color of dried cornstalks. The boy, who looked to be slightly younger than Jody, was Black. He wore a baseball cap backward on his head, and for some reason he wore mittens, though it was summer. His features were bunched in an expression of pure rage, as if he were just looking for someone to provoke him into a fight.

"Did you know a brontosaurus weighed like seventy-seven thousand pounds?" Jody announced out of the blue. Instead of addressing me, she spoke directly to the boy across from her, who only glared in response.

"Really?" I tried to make up for the boy's icy manner with my own enthusiasm. "That's incredible!"

"Yep. And it only ate vegetables!"

"You mean it was a vegetarian?"

"It loved to eat. It ate all day." She was still talking to the boy, who, in his quiet seething, appeared to take every word as a direct offense. I crinkled my newspaper in an attempt to distract Jody, but she kept chatting. "It just ate and ate and ate and ate." She made tearing and chewing motions with her mouth. "It mostly hung out in the water near the shore. Wanna know why? Because it was too fat to stand up on land. What a fatso! Except not for its brain. Its brain weighed, get this, just one pound."

"Just one pound!" I echoed.

She bounced on the cushion and in her excitement kicked the woman, who glanced coldly at me to register her indignation.

"Jody," I whispered, taking her wrist. "Please."

She fell back into her seat, and I released her and returned to the newspaper. The train was rolling slowly, grinding along the track past repairmen. Jody waved at them as we passed. One of the men waved back. The train inched along. I absorbed myself for a few minutes in an article about the rising prices of real estate. When we came to a full halt, I looked through the circle on the window. We had stopped in an underpass; on the concrete wall someone had spelled out the word HERO in dripping orange paint.

My attention moved to Jody, and I noticed only then what was happening. Jody was staring at the boy across from her, and the boy was staring back, the children locked in a contest that I worried could only end badly, the two of them barely breathing, the woman in charge of the boy making notations in her notebook, oblivious to the children as each tried to make the other blink, both of them set on nothing less than a victory that could only be humiliating to the loser.

"Jody," I said in a low voice. "Jody, if you don't want to go to the zoo, where do you want to go?"

The woman across from me busily scratched away with her pencil; the train started moving again with a jerk; the two children went on staring, rigid as statues.

"Jody!" I hissed.

She refused to acknowledge me. I watched in dismay as she filled her mouth with a gradual intake of breath, bloating her cheeks and forcing her pupils together in cross-eyed concentration. She held the pose for so long that she grew red in the face. I feared that she would cause herself to faint, and I was about to offer a friendly poke in her cheek to deflate her when the boy suddenly erupted, throwing himself backward against the seat and squealing with uncontrollable laughter. And then Jody was laughing, too, wiggling and bouncing and laughing. The sight of two small children laughing hysterically caused the woman across from me to giggle, and then I couldn't help it, I was laughing too, and then the couple across the aisle from us started laughing, and then the conductor passing through to collect our ticket stubs joined in the laughter. The whole train car was shaking with glee as we pulled into a tunnel, the darkness forming a backdrop behind the window, the interior light illuminating the dust lines of the smiling face on the glass.

By the end of the journey, my ribs ached from all the hilarity. I composed myself, folding the newspaper and checking my purse to make sure it was snapped shut. I gave a friendly nod to the woman across from me to indicate that she and the boy could enter the aisle ahead of us. She reached for the boy's hand and inadvertently pulled off his mitten. I looked quickly away, but a glance had been enough to see that the boy's skin was badly scarred with swollen raw-pink crescents, most likely from some terrible burn. The boy was too happy to care about his injury right then, too carefree to be self-conscious. He was wobbling his head and sticking out his tongue at Jody as the woman tucked his hand back in the mitten. Jody laughed again, and the boy laughed. He was still laughing as the woman tugged him along the platform, and they disappeared into the crowd.

"If you don't want to go to the zoo, where do you want to go? Jody? Hello, Jody, earth to Jody."

We were strolling aimlessly on the sidewalk, surrounded by women carrying shopping bags, packs of teenagers all wearing embroidered bell-bottoms, couples holding hands. It was a holiday weekend, and the stores were advertising sales. A horse-drawn carriage shared the street with taxis. There was cigar smoke, exhaust, and the smell of manure in the air.

We stopped to buy a hot pretzel, and I convinced the vendor to sell it to us for a quarter instead of the thirty cents he tried to charge us. I wanted to show Jody how business transpired in the city, to teach her to be savvy and prepare her for the tough competition in life.

We had just crossed a side street when Jody stopped. I thought she was bending down to tie her sneaker. No, she was leaning toward a homeless man propped up against the wall of the building. The two stumps of his legs, amputated at the knees, extended in front of him. Draped in an army overcoat, he was holding a sign: HUNGRY. His upturned baseball cap on the sidewalk was already full of coins.

Back then I was working as an editorial assistant and during the week commuted into the city. I kept loose change in my purse just so I wouldn't have to fumble with my wallet when I wanted to help out a panhandler. Usually I would make some paltry contribution and move on as quickly as possible to avoid contemplating humanity's inequities. But that day with Jody, it didn't occur to me to reach for change, because I was too appalled by what Jody was doing. Before I could stop her, Jody offered her half-eaten pretzel to the man, a gesture that I was sure would be registered as insulting and provoke, I predicted, a barrage of obscenities, or worse. I grabbed her arm and led her away.

I was as wrong about the man as I'd been about the boy on the train. The man held the half loop of the pretzel high, as if in victory. "Bless you, child!" he called to Jody. With his free hand, he blew Jody a kiss. Jody stretched out her arm as if holding a baseball mitt, then made a show of tucking the kiss she'd caught safely in the back pocket of her overalls.

It was Jody who decided she wanted to visit the Cloisters that day. I was surprised that a little girl would choose the Cloisters over the Children's Zoo, but I didn't try to talk her out of it. We took the M4 uptown, and we were inside the museum by noon, sitting at a table in a stone corridor, eating self-service cheese sandwiches and looking over a map of the galleries.

We started out in one of the gardens, where Jody spent a long time sniffing the different herbs growing below the quince trees and comparing their fragrances, trying to decide which she liked best. She admired the wild creatures that were carved into pink stone capitals. In the Glass Gallery, she wondered about the roundel depicting a king perched atop a patchwork horse. She thought it funny that the king was pointing at something ahead of him while his two servants were looking in the opposite direction.

In a small gallery adjacent to a chapel, we found ourselves surrounded by members of a large tour. The docent was speaking loudly, lecturing about the paintings in the room, and we stuck around long enough to learn from her why in one of the paintings, a saint was holding a cittern, and in another painting, a saint was holding a book. We learned that backgrounds were painted gold to make them visible in candlelight. We heard stories of martyrs and prophets and were encouraged to look closely to see secret symbols.

Jody seemed in no hurry to leave the gallery, even after the tour group moved on. There was one painting in particular, hung low on the wall, that caught her attention. It was an oil portrait on wood. Inside the heavy gilt frame was a portrait of a woman, her almond eyes heavily outlined in black, her dark brows curved, her nose exceptionally long and narrow. The face was stiff and unnaturally elongated, making it look mask-like. I wouldn't have thought the painting would be of any interest to a six-year-old girl, until Jody called my attention to the one detail that I had to agree was quite striking: a teardrop, perfectly realistic, on the woman's cheek.

Jody's finger reached precariously close to the portrait. Remember that back then there were no electronic motion detectors protecting paintings. There wasn't even a dedicated museum guard in that particular gallery. The nearest guard was stationed inside the doorway leading into the adjacent chapel.

I pulled Jody's arm away from the painting and encouraged her to take a step back. At a safe distance, we stood side by side, examining the teardrop. I wondered how a tiny drop of paint, a visible bump on the wood, could so convincingly render the transparency of a tear. I was fascinated and yet, for some reason I can't explain, troubled by its illusion. The effect of the tear was like a clock's quiet ticking in a dark room, and the longer I stood there, the more unsettled I felt.

"How about we go to the gift shop?" I suggested. "You can pick out something for yourself. My treat." Without waiting for Jody to respond, I took her hand and led her from the gallery.

We stopped in a nearby restroom, and when Jody finished drying her hands ahead of me I asked her to wait out in the corridor. I took an extra minute to reapply my lipstick, and then went out, expecting to find Jody beside the door. But Jody wasn't there. I looked up and down the crowded corridor, then returned into the restroom and called her name. She did not answer. A toilet flushed, and from a stall emerged an elderly woman in a pillbox hat. I went back out into the corridor, my panic growing as I called for my niece, my voice rising loud enough to cause strangers to turn around in search of the disruption.

I thought Jody might have misunderstood my instruction to wait out in the corridor and had gone on her own to the gift shop. But she didn't know where the gift shop was. I considered how easily distracted she was. Maybe she had followed another docent's tour, or gone outside to smell the herbs again. Could someone have lured her away? She was a little girl who lacked the ability to recognize danger. No, I corrected myself—she may have been overly friendly, but she wasn't stupid. Most likely, a security guard had spotted her and recognized that she was too young to be on her own. Where was the room where they brought lost children?

One thought pounded out the next as I rushed across the Chapter House, down a corridor and through the chapel and into the garden. I could hear the honking of impatient drivers on the street beyond the walls, and, further in the distance, the whine of a siren. I ran back through a corridor, stopping to check every gallery. I tried to be reasonable, telling myself that Jody must be nearby even as I feared the worst. I had lost my sister's daughter. My bestest niece. Dear, sweet Jody.

"Jody, there you are!"

If I had been thinking clearly, I would have known exactly where I would find her—back in the last gallery where we had lingered to gaze at the dot of a teardrop.

"You gave me a scare!" I said, even as I became aware that the elderly woman in the pillbox hat was staring at us from across the room, as if we were the ones on exhibit. I lowered my voice to a whisper. "Don't ever disappear like that again, Jody!"

"Sorry." Her attention was now on her hands, perhaps so she wouldn't have to meet my reproachful gaze. Her lower lip was curled in a pout, and with her thumbnail she picked at dirt underneath the nail of her index finger. I decided to give her an extra minute to feel remorseful and bided time by looking back at the painting, taking in the entirety of the portrait, thinking again that the face was like a mask, unreal except for that very real teardrop that was no more than a pimple of silver paint.

No, not even a pimple. In place of the teardrop was a flat, scratched blankness. A fuzzy nothing that reminded me of the shadow left behind when a candy button is peeled off its paper ribbon.

I looked at Jody, who was working at her fingernail, trying to pry free a fleck of dirt. I understood in an instant what she'd done. Beneath her sharp fingernail was a minuscule silver chip of bone-dry, ancient paint—a pimple of paint.

Jody, I didn't say aloud, we better get out of here! I just grabbed the little hand containing that six-hundred-year-old teardrop, and I led my niece from the gallery, past the woman in the pillbox hat and into the crowded corridor, down the marble stairs, and out onto the street.

I used to be assiduous at keeping a personal journal. The record of my life consisted of a daily paragraph or two written in my sloppy handwriting, sometimes in pencil, more often in pen, in one of the spiral notebooks that are now gathering dust in my attic. I don't know why I even keep them around. Rarely do I bother to read what I wrote, for I am apprehensive about what I may learn. I don't like to be reminded of unful-filled dreams, love affairs that ended badly, tests I failed, job interviews that came to nothing. I don't want to see that the entries written in pencil have faded so much they are largely illegible. Regarding that day in June of 1965 when I treated my little niece to a trip to the city while her mother was in the hospital, I would rather forget how hard I was on my brother-in-law. Perusing words committed to paper fifty years ago, I wince at my vindictive charge that my sister's illness was her husband's fault. I am embarrassed at how oblivious I was to my own shortcomings. I read with disbelief about my indignation, my impatience and false assumptions.

My sister, in fact, would heal and go on to live a good life in remission for another twenty years, happily married to Jody's father, who, shortly after his wife came home from the hospital, would get himself to an AA meeting and spend the rest of his life sober. Jody was destined to grow up and have two daughters of her own and work as a psychologist before succumbing at the age of sixty-three to the same cancer that afflicted her mother. At a New Year's Eve party shortly before her death, she would ask me, "Auntie, do you remember that day you took me to the Cloisters when Mom was in the hospital?"

How could I forget! In fact, it turned out to be too easy for each of us to forget in our selective ways. I would gather from Jody that while she remembered the staring contest with the boy on the train, along with certain other details of the day, she had no recollection of her act of vandalism, and I was not inclined to remind her. Concerning that particular incident, my memory is infallible. Other events of that day, however—my success at reducing the cost of a pretzel, for instance—would be lost to oblivion if I had not provided an account in my journal—luckily, in pen.

* * *

On the train home that day in 1965, I didn't bother to impress upon Jody the magnitude of her crime. I resolved to keep it a secret for the child's sake, and for the sake of her beleaguered parents. On a subsequent visit to the Cloisters the following month, I discreetly returned to the gallery to check on the painting, but it had been removed from the wall and replaced with a coat of arms. As far as I know, the painting of the weeping woman was never exhibited again.

Jody, meanwhile, would continue to be driven by an insatiable desire to relieve other people of the burden of their sorrows. To the end of her life, her inability to tolerate sadness was as much a fixed trait as the color of her hair, and it accounted for both her cheerful, loving spirit and an impulsiveness she never fully learned to restrain.

Let me, though, take full responsibility for the damaged painting. I was the one who brought Jody to the Cloisters, and I was the one who lost track of her. I chose to protect her with my silence. Only in her absence, after we buried her next to her mother, was I ready to make a full confession. And so, last month, I put my testimony in a letter addressed to the director of the museum, and then I sat back and waited for my punishment.

You can imagine my surprise when I received no reply. I had confessed to covering up an act of outrageous vandalism; I was ready to endure the consequences. At the very least, I expected that the museum would demand compensation for the damaged painting. Perhaps my letter had never reached the director. I picked up the phone and called his office. I told my story to an assistant, who, after hearing me out, put me on hold while she checked the catalogue. Back on the line, she reported the museum had no listing of any work of art in their collection that matched the painting I described.

"Ma'am, you must be mistaken," she blithely insisted.

I asked to speak to her boss. Oddly, the assistant put me through to the Department of External Affairs. What did my story have to do with External Affairs? They wondered the same thing and put me on hold. I was referred from one staff member to another, until I reached someone in a curatorial department, who confirmed once and for all that the painting I described had never existed.

"Really!" I couldn't contain my irritation. "Do you think I just made up this whole story? How about I put it in print and we let the public decide?"

Which brings me to my current predicament. Unable to verify this story but determined to publish it, I have been instructed by legal experts to pretend that any resemblance to real persons is entirely coincidental. Gone is the truth, along with that dried-up drop of paint. Believe what you will. I'll just say that it is not the first time a museum has lost track of an item in its collection. Maybe the damaged painting was destroyed, or it was stolen, or it was discreetly used to repay a debt. My guess is that in one of the unused bedrooms of some mansion hidden at the end of a long, gated drive is a portrait of a weeping woman who sheds no tears.

Infidels

I t was a damp November afternoon in Paris in 1887 when the man who would be identified in the book only as "C" suffered the first symptoms of the affliction that would make him noteworthy. He had risen from his nap and settled comfortably into his armchair by the window overlooking the Place des Vosges. Droplets from the thick fog ran like tears down the exterior of the glass. A wood fire crackled and filled the room with its soothing fragrance.[*]

Long married but with no heirs, recently retired from a position as director of a champagne export business, C

---

[*] I came across the story of C when I was browsing at a used bookstore in Ithaca. I read the case history while standing in the aisle. Stupidly, I left without purchasing the book. When I returned for it later, the book was gone. I don't recall the title. C's story, however, left an indelible impression in my mind.

did not lack for friends. He and his wife dined out most evenings, and he was an active member of the Société de Géographie. But C also guarded his solitude and spent most of his afternoons alone in his library. He was well-educated and fluent in several languages. He longed to author something of his own but didn't know how to begin. He was secretly critical of contemporary men of letters and blamed novelists, especially, for pandering to the public and emptying their work of useful information. The worst of them, in his opinion, was Victor Hugo, who used to live in an apartment across the square. C had read a couple of novels and a book of verse by his former neighbor. He wasn't inclined to read more. He wasn't at all curious. What was there to be curious about if there was nothing to learn? He had read enough to reach the verdict that the whole of Hugo's oeuvre was overrated.

In general, he preferred reading biographies and military histories. On this particular day in 1887, we find him reading a volume he had purchased for a few francs from a bookseller near the Pont Marie. It was an English edition about the Crusades, and C was reading with interest about the disorder in the ranks of the early Christian pilgrims.[*]

"The vulgar, both the great and small, were taught to believe every wonder, of lands flowing with milk and honey," he read.

---

[*] The book C was reading consisted of late chapters extracted from Edward Gibbon's classic work and republished in a pocket edition titled simply *The Crusades*. I have checked the quotes for accuracy.

"Their ignorance of the country, or war, and of discipline exposed them to every snare," he read.

"A pyramid of bones informed their companions of the place of their defeat," he read, and he continued to read the sentence stating that "three hundred thousand had already perished before a single city was rescued from the—"

And then he stopped, or was stopped, as if he had run with his eyes closed into a brick wall. His eyes were wide open, but he couldn't read the word that followed in the sentence. The word was *infidels*. It should have been a familiar word to C even if he hadn't been entirely fluent in English, since it was nearly identical in French: *infidèles*. He knew the word in English just as he knew it in French. He knew it in Latin and Spanish. Really, it should have been easy enough for C to comprehend. Yet, to his dismay, the word was utterly unintelligible. His eyes processed the letters in their correct order. His brain received the information in the usual fashion. He inhaled, and his oxygenated blood flowed briskly. All organs were seemingly in working order, and C was very much awake, utterly sober and self-aware, but the eight letters of that English word were as devoid of meaning as if he had never learned to read.

It's true that many of us have experienced the odd momentary sensation when a simple word is suddenly unrecognizable. Scientists call this phenomenon "semantic satiation" and explain it as a result of overuse of a specific neural pattern. They hypothesize that intense repetition of a specific word creates a reactive inhibition, slowing the neural activity associated with the meaning of that word. We can read the word *want,* for instance, without difficulty. But reading it over and over interferes with comprehension: *want want want want want want want want want want want want want want want want.*[*]

This, however, was not what C experienced that day in 1887. He didn't perceive the word as a familiar one that he'd once known. The letters were so unrecognizable that *infidel* wasn't even a word to him. It was a solid blankness, a splotch of spilled ink, an absolute nothing.

He removed his spectacles, rubbed them with his handkerchief, and returned them to his face. The one printed word he didn't recognize became two, and two seeped into a sentence. He squinted and shifted in his chair. He opened the window shade. He tried to reread the preceding paragraph. With relief, he experienced some recognition: he knew what *pyramid* signified, and *bones,* and *defeat.* Yes, he knew what each of those words meant, thank God. *Pyramid, bones, defeat.*

Awareness was painfully brief. *Py…ra…, bo…n…, defe…a….* It was as if the light within each letter went out one by one, until each word was dark.

---

[*]   One study has gone so far as to suggest that the recent dramatic uptick in this phenomenon is due to the simplification of writing necessitated by mobile devices. Smaller screens demand a smaller vocabulary, increasing both our exposure to a smaller number of words and the concurrent increase in semantic satiation. See T. Leonardo, S. Pissoralüpa, and J. M. Merendeskewski, "Neurosemantic Frequency Patterning in ERP DHA Measured Outcomes," *Journal of Neuromorphological Studies* 1752, nos. 2–3 (2018): 132–45.

With rising concern, he turned to words in his native language. He tried and failed to read the front page of the newspaper that lay open on his desk. The titles of the books on his shelves were unintelligible. He couldn't even read the name printed on his own stationery.

Naturally, he consulted his doctor. His doctor referred him to a specialist, who would go on to study him with interest and publish his case history. That C retained his speaking fluency gave the scientific community much to ponder. If you had conversed with him, you wouldn't have seen signs of his impairment, which affected only his perception of printed words. In other ways, he lived a normal life.

For our purposes, however, it is enough to know that once C fully lost his ability to read, he never recovered it. I won't even bother telling you about his first appointment with his doctor. What concerns us here is C's adventure that day after he decided that all he needed was a good, brisk walk around the square to clear his confused mind.

Back in the early 1980s, when I was a student studying in Paris, I used to make my way to the Place des Vosges to get away from the bustle of the city. I remember how the streams of clear water gushed from the mouths of stone lions in the central fountain, and the groomed lawns bordered by metal wickets looked as perfect as if they'd been painted green. Linden trees grew in stately rows. An artificial hush seemed to mute the noise of traffic on the adjacent streets, as if a volume dial had been adjusted.

It was a warm spring that year, and I would sit on a bench and enjoy the sunlight on my face. One day, I fell into conversation with an old woman who was feeding crumbs to the pigeons. She saw my backpack and identified me as an American. She asked if I liked Paris. I said I liked it very much. She asked if I liked the Place des Vosges. I said I thought it was beautiful. Though the sky was clear, the woman wore a tan raincoat that was oversized on her small frame. Her cheeks had the deep creases of leather boots that had gone unworn for decades. She was eager to talk, and I was glad to have the chance to practice my French. When she asked, out of the blue, if I believed in ghosts, I said, "*Oui, madame,*" just to play along.

And so it was from this old woman that I learned something about the bloody history of the Place des Vosges. Long ago, she explained to me as she tore off pinches of bread to toss to the birds, the large square was occupied by the Palais des Tournelles, named for numerous turrets that decorated its rim. It was here, in the courtyard of the palace, that Henri II was wounded in a tilting match with the Duke of Montgomery, whose spear splintered against the king's visor, sending shards through his eyes and into his brain. The king suffered for eleven days in painful agony before finally dying. In mourning, his wife, Catherine de' Medici, ordered the palace to be destroyed.

This is where a ghost enters the story: the old woman claimed the Place des Vosges was haunted by Henri II. I asked her whether she had ever seen the king herself. "*Bien sûr!"* she said. It was impossible to predict when he would make an appearance. Some said he came on the nights when Venus was closest to earth, while others maintained that he could be seen during a lunar eclipse, or on the anniversary of his death, or birth, or marriage. He would appear in his suit of armor walking slowly across the grass to the fountain. He would remove his helmet with his broken visor and dip his hands into the water being spit out by one of the stone lions. He would wash the blood from his face, then he would put his helmet back on and walk away.

The old woman was fourteen years old when she had first seen him, on her way home from a tavern where she worked sweeping the floors. She had seen him three times since then. With a theatrical grimace, she tried to convey how frightening he was to behold. When her lips peeled back, I noticed that she was missing several upper molars.

I didn't bother to wait around to see if the ghost of Henri II would make his entrance that evening. It had become increasingly obvious to me that the woman was suffering from senility. I could only hope that she was receiving adequate care. As for me, though I appreciate a good ghost story, I thought I could tell the difference between fiction and fact—until I stumbled across the story of C.

My sense of C is that he was even more of a skeptic than yours truly. Though he was a dutiful Catholic and went to confession once a week, he much preferred forms of knowledge that could be verified. When in doubt, he would always side with replicable proof. As for human attempts to expose the secrets of mortality, he believed that the truth was visible in every corpse: you could see just by looking at a man without a heartbeat that death was the end of life. There was no world elsewhere. C was convinced that heaven and hell existed only as imagined places. His pragmatic mind had no room for phantoms.

The fog that had settled over the city of Paris the day C lost his ability to read was so dense, and the winter dusk had come so early, that he could barely make out the outlines of the tall buildings across the square. He felt the unnerving sensation of being lost, though he knew exactly where he was. He resisted the urge to grab the arm of a woman who was walking ahead of him along the gravel path. Feathers sticking up from the bulb of her hat shook in the swirling mist. C gasped, mistaking the feathers for a live bird. He took a few steps backward and would have stumbled, but luckily his hand found the iron armrest of a bench. He lowered himself onto the seat. With a few deep breaths, he was able to calm his agitation.

The quiet of the square had a restorative effect, and he began to appreciate the peculiar beauty of the fog. It would have been fine weather for spectral illusions. C smiled at the thought. Of course he'd heard the silly stories about Henri II. He enjoyed the feeling of superiority that overcame him when he considered how susceptible other people were to superstition, how easily they would mistake a tree trunk, blurred by the heavy cloud, for the ghost of a dead king.

He tipped his head back and closed his eyes. Voices of passersby seemed to come from far away. He could almost fancy that he was at the seashore. He found himself remembering the sensation he'd loved so much when he was a young boy and let the gentle waves wash the sand over his toes.

A nearby cough had the startling effect of shattering glass. C blinked. That's when he noticed the man at the opposite end of the bench. He didn't know how long the man had been there—probably he had just arrived. He wore an old-fashioned sack suit with a tailcoat that was unbuttoned, revealing a plaid vest and the froth of a white ruffled shirt. His black cravat was tied in a bow and brushed against the rough curls of his white beard. He had a pencil out and was writing on a piece of paper. His expression had the fixed aspect of a statue and gave little indication of his thoughts. From C's perspective, there was a melancholy air about the man, a perfuse, sad loneliness that kept him helplessly sealed off from the rest of humanity.

C tried not to stare. There was something familiar about the stranger; a moment of reflection brought clear identification as C recognized his former neighbor, Victor Hugo.

Victor Hugo!

But that was impossible—Victor Hugo was dead. He had been dead for two years. C had been inconvenienced by the author's huge funeral procession in front of the Panthéon.

Oh, but it was him, there was no denying. Victor Hugo, buried in a tomb he shared with Zola and Dumas, was sitting beside C on an iron bench in the Place des Vosges. C was overtaken by a clarity of mind that came in stark contrast to the confusion he'd experienced earlier. He could no longer find meaning in printed words, but he could see reality for what it was.

Hugo brought the back of his hand to his mouth and coughed again. He was old and haggard, but his poor health couldn't stop him from scribbling on the paper. C felt a wave of pity for Hugo and wanted to reach out to him and tell him…what? What could he possibly say? He searched his memory for a passage from one of Hugo's verses. Instead, a scene from the famous early novel about the hunchback came to mind. He remembered the passage almost word for word. He remembered how Djali, the little pet goat of La Esmeralda, gets his horns tangled in the folds of a noblewoman's dress. C's heart ached as he thought of all the ugly, contemptuous aristocrats mocking La Esmeralda, calling her a witch and ordering her to make the goat perform a feat of magic.

C wasn't prone to sentimentality, but who could resist when the actors on the page were so vividly rendered? It occurred to him that he had judged Hugo's work too harshly through the years. His inclination to find faults had dominated his reading experience. He realized that in his urge to be critical, he had missed the sheer, absorbing pleasure of Hugo's books. Why, he had only to gaze at the sad, decrepit ghost beside him and realize that his stories would survive the eroding effects of time. Centuries would pass, and the books would continue to be read…though not by C, since C could no longer read.[*]

Awareness filled him with horror. He would never again be able to read about La Esmeralda disentangling Djali's horns from Madame Aloïse's dress! He didn't need a doctor to examine him to conclude with absolute certainty that his impairment was permanent. Printed words forever on would be impenetrable. If he wanted to read, he would have to be read to. It wasn't the same when the words were spoken aloud. No, it wasn't at all the same as digesting words visually and letting them transport him far from his armchair into a world illuminated by the light of his solitary consciousness. He had failed to fully savor the distinct satisfaction that comes with reading selflessly, propelled by selfless interest. All through his adult life, when his intellect was at its sharpest, he had positioned himself in competition with the books in his library. Now it was too late to start over. He had missed his chance.

Casting a sorrowful glance at C, Victor Hugo stood, fluffed out the tails of his coat, and walked away. C resisted calling out to him. He watched silently as the ghost dissolved in the mist. After Victor Hugo had disappeared entirely, C bravely fought against despair and invited a return of cold common sense. He told himself that he had imagined the whole

---

[*] C was probably wrong about the survival of Victor Hugo's books. Predictive patterns based on data by Leonardo et al. (ibid.) indicate that by the year 2150, the majority of the human species will be illiterate.

encounter. There had been no ghost. He said it over and over to himself: There had been no ghost!

He would have been persuaded if he hadn't seen, beside him on the bench, the piece of paper Victor Hugo had left behind. C was reluctant to pick it up. It would cause him too much distress, since he wouldn't be able to read what Hugo had written. It would only be painful to peruse the scrawl of ink and fail to make sense of it. Hugo had probably written something brilliant; C would never know. He would leave the paper there. He would not allow himself to be tormented. But an unusual curiosity overtook him, and he gingerly lifted a corner of the paper.

He was able to perceive an entangled confection made of graphite. It took extra scrutiny in the dim light to realize he was looking not at words, but at a drawing. At first it seemed a busy patterned design, flowers tumbling behind a web, but on further consideration he came to see the circles, one dark, one hollow, that represented eyes, and a grim, skewed oval of a mouth lined with monstrous teeth, and wisps of a beard trailing like Medusa's snakes. C finally recognized in the image the shape of a ghostly face, dissolving into a net of lines, as if printed on lace.

Victor Hugo had left behind a drawing. This was his gift to C, who from that day on could no longer read but could still see with perfect clarity. In the picture Victor Hugo had made in C's presence, C saw the self-portrait of the very ghost with whom he had shared the bench. It did not take much effort to see that the illustration succeeded in capturing all the mysterious brilliance of the artist on a single sheet of paper. He was filled with admiration and at the same time he perceived in the image the full imaginative depths he'd missed in the previous years. It felt as if he were looking through ice at a spectacular underwater garden.

The effect of the drawing was so disorienting that in the days to come C would put it in a drawer, out of sight. Anyway, medical examinations and experimental treatments would keep him so busy he wouldn't have time for anything else. He decided that rather than leave the drawing to languish in his desk, he would donate it to the city of Paris. When the Victor Hugo Museum was established on the Place des Vosges in 1902, it would be displayed among the author's papers in a second-floor gallery. It remains there to this day. I know, for I have seen it myself.

No One Is Available

M y friend Alexander, a retired physics professor, could be found on any given day wandering among the stacks of the library, selecting books at random. He read law journals, outdated computer coding guides, chapbooks of poetry from the 1800s, forgotten novels, memoirs of kings and explorers and prostitutes, books about subjects as varied as Byzantine mosaics, Victorian prisons, clock repair, and Scottish epitaphs. His favorite place to while away the seasons was the library basement, tucked in at a wooden carrel thickly carved with obscenities and pronouncements of love.

During his prime years as a scientist, he concentrated his research on the aerodynamics of raindrops, though he never did more than confirm results from other physicists' experiments. He had a lover who died of cancer in 1985, and he has been single ever since. For pets he hosted generations of goldfish. He used to play tennis regularly, but in his emeritus years he was content just to sit and read all day. When we met for our daily pint, he held forth on what he had read most recently, describing content in fascinating detail without ever seeming boorish.

I suppose it makes sense that a man who was such a passionate reader would one day decide to write a book himself. But though I pressed him on it, he refused to tell me what his book was going to be about, even whether it was to be based on fantasy or fact. Perhaps he intended to write a novel in verse, I joked, receiving in reply no more than a shrug. Was there one particular work that had lit the fuse of his ambition? He wouldn't say. I pointed out that all his writing up to that point had been done for scientific journals and in collaboration with his fellow researchers; he'd never written anything on his own. It didn't matter. Once he'd made up his mind he was fully dedicated to the notion.

He gave up the library carrel and set up his office in his house. He purchased an antique pedestal desk with stacked drawers, sharpened the points on a dozen No. 2 pencils, fixed corner tabs on his desk to frame a composition book, and opened to the first page. He knew what he wanted to write but had no idea how to begin. Now, with everything in place, my friend waited for the first words to come to him. He waited patiently through the whole day. He waited in the same fashion the next day. Days turned to weeks, and he was still waiting.

Three months later, he woke early, before his alarm clock went off. It was an overcast morning, and the grayness muted the brightening dawn. Alexander knew immediately what he would write; indeed, he saw his book in his mind word for word, as if the whole of it were contained on a chalkboard in front of him, like a mathematical solution. He could hardly wait to get going, though he also knew the importance of patience. With methodical care, he made himself rich dark coffee using Japanese paper and a porcelain filter. He ate a buttered English muffin, with penny slices of banana on the side. He used the toilet, then showered, brushed his teeth, exchanged his bathrobe for jeans and a T-shirt, and went up to his office.

He turned on the overhead light and situated his chair appropriately. A bamboo shade covered the upper half of the room's single window. It might or might not be significant that the dictionary on the left side of his desk happened to be open to the page ending with the word *charismata,* and a magnifying glass placed at an angle over the page captured half of the long definition of the word *charge.*

He rolled a pencil fondly between his thumb and forefinger. He touched the tip to the paper. He wrote, "As she looked up at the arms of the masthead..."

And then the phone rang, the sound like boiling water dumped on his head. The tip of the pencil broke. The phone kept ringing and ringing. Alexander picked up the receiver. A misfiring robotic voice announced, "No one is available to take your call at the moment," an attempt, it appeared, to field an inquiry that had never been initiated.

"No one is available to take your call at the moment, no one is available to take your call at the moment," the robot taunted, until Alexander hung up.

He was normally an upbeat fellow and wasn't used to feeling so annoyed. He tried to resume where he'd left off, but now he could hear children cannonballing into his neighbor's pool, along with the whirring and beeping of a truck collecting refuse on the street. No matter how hard he tried through the hours and days that followed, he couldn't recover a single word. The book he had barely started was lost forever.

Have you ever been interrupted in your work? Do you know what it feels like when your concentration is shattered by unwanted interference, and the thread of a promising idea is snapped? Has a person like the person from Porlock ever knocked on your door, as he reputedly did at Coleridge's cottage in Nether Stowey, perhaps, it's been speculated, to deliver laudanum, or maybe to collect on a debt? Have you never, like my friend, or Coleridge, dreamed of something more perfect than anything you could have come up with when you were awake? Can we even claim that Coleridge's intended poem truly exists in its incomplete state? Isn't it more accurate to say that the poem resulting from the interruption is a wholly different poem from the one Coleridge would have written if he'd been left alone, and that the unwritten "Kubla Khan" sits beside the printed version like a long evening shadow?

When Alexander told me about his attempt to write a book, he would assume responsibility not just for failing but for presuming he could be a writer in the first place. It was stupid of him ever to think he could master language sufficiently to fill a whole book. As for the story of his life, he could sum it up in a paragraph. His brain was too packed with equations to allow much room for his personal memories. He was a numbers guy, and while he admired the ingenuity of writers, verbal manipulation was never his thing. It had always bugged him that dictionaries are so fat, there are so many different words with interchangeable meanings, and anyway, readers are understandably impatient, no one lingers over every painstakingly thought-up sentence, in truth he hadn't wanted to waste even a fraction of his life on something that probably would have resulted in public embarrassment, and when the phone rang he was already looking for a reason to turn back before he was too far gone. All in all, he said, he was grateful for the interruption. From then on, he would stick to science.

"Give me dry friction," he shouted on the one occasion he got visibly drunk. "Give me centripetal acceleration! Give me gravity and torque and incontrovertible data!"

We clinked pints, laughing together at his foolishness. I have to admit, though, that even as I was sucking foam from my beer I was wondering if maybe my friend underestimated himself. I would have liked to read what he came up with. I wonder what he would have revealed if he had gone on to write a book. I know this man. I have experience of his brilliance, his supple, open-minded approach to problems, his vivacity, his sensitivity. I keep trying to guess what he would have written. Would he have offered a new way of thinking about familiar experience? Could it be that his research on raindrops would have given him a unique insight into life? I guess we'll never know.

The Palimpsest

The Codex Kraos Ephrip'tus, or Codex K.E. as it came to be called, was an unusual object. The original text consisted of dense lettering packed into a single column per page and punctuated with filigreed capitals. The pages were parchment sewn together; the wooden cover was decorated with dollops of melted gold. Rumored to contain recipes for performing miracles, including detailed instructions for bringing the dead back to life, it was written in a forgotten Arcadian dialect that no one could read. The book was treasured and preserved mainly because of the cover, though there was hope that one day a scholar would come along who could translate the writing.

In the eleventh century, in the library of the Amanoriotissa monastery, a nearsighted scribe opened the Codex K.E.

Concluding that the faded writing would never be legible, he decided to recycle the parchment and put it to a better purpose. He brushed a thin wash over the vestiges of ink, and he filled the newly blank parchment with select passages from the Greek Bible.

We know that a monk named Pamphilos carried the Codex K.E. with him when he fled the sacking of Smyrna by Tamerlane in 1402. The story has it that his ship was wrecked in a storm, and pirates found him drifting on a makeshift raft on the open sea. They took him on board and assigned him the hard task of emptying the bilge buckets. Pamphilos sailed with the pirates for two years, until he managed to sneak away while supplies were being loaded in an inlet near Ancona. He wandered for miles, carrying the book in his sack, and finally found refuge in an abandoned shepherd's hut. He took ill and died there, and for years the codex was lost.

In 1478, a boy searching for a lost sheep discovered the ruins of the hut. He climbed the one portion of the wall that was still standing, and while looking out over the field, he slipped and fell, hitting his head on a stone. As he regained consciousness, his gaze settled on the corner of a metal box that was partially visible beneath the rubble. The box, it turned out, contained the Codex K.E. Although a gray mold had discolored much of the parchment, the binding and cover were still intact, and there was an insert that contained details of the book's provenance.

After much discussion among the boy's relatives, it was

decided that the codex should be delivered to Cosimo de' Medici, who was famous for, among other things, his love of books. The boy's uncle was appointed as emissary and made his way to Florence without incident, putting the Codex K.E. in the hands of Cosimo himself. But the uncle failed to return to the palace for his promised reward, and he never arrived home in Ancona. The mystery of his fate remains unresolved to this day. Some speculate that he got drunk and drowned in the Arno, others that he was murdered by the Medici guards in order to save Cosimo the cost of the reward.

The Codex K.E. joined other rare manuscripts in the vaults of the palace. It went unread for years, until it was selected as one of the gifts to Catherine de' Medici, in celebration of her marriage to Henri II of France. She had little interest in the book but was obliged to carry it with her to Paris, where it was examined by the royal chaplain, who resolved to have the biblical passages transcribed. The process was painstaking, but eventually a fair copy was completed, and the codex was filed away in the library at Fontainebleau.

Decades stretched into centuries. Finally, in 1742, an esteemed scholar who had long been familiar with the rumors about the secret contents of the Codex K.E. asked to examine it. As it happened, a beam of sunlight shone through a high window at such an angle that it lit up the parchment, revealing, below the surface, the shadows of inked lines and feathery curlicues. The man suspected at once what he was seeing: these were the legendary instructions for performing miracles, written in a forgotten language that he was sure he could decode, if only the lettering were clear enough to be deciphered.

In a daguerreotype I have of my great-great-grandfather Hercule, he is a boy, dressed in knickerbockers and a matching jacket fastened at the neck, trimmed with braids and buttons. A banded cap is perched on his head like a saucer. His lips are pressed tightly together, his cheeks puffed and dented with the Fourniers' signature dimples. You don't need to know the family stories about him to see that the boy in the daguerreotype has a mischievous glint in his eye. Clearly, he was a rascal who loved practical jokes. My hunch is that my great-great-grandfather had been told that he mustn't smile while the daguerreotypist was capturing his image, and his form of protest was to fill his cheeks with air and slowly emit a farting sound—that's what we'd hear, I bet, if the daguerreotype came with audio.

According to the family lore, it was decided by his parents that Hercule would be trained in the apothecary profession. In preparation, he was sent to work for Monsieur Lambertine, a renowned chemist and inventor of a solution used to clean paints from zinc blocks. *Tinctura lambertina* was popular with lithographers who were churning out colored advertisements and playing cards at the time. The patent made Lambertine a small fortune, and his laboratory functioned like a factory. Lambertine employed six apprentices, who prepared great vats of his signature potion for sale. Two boys were in charge of pounding minerals into dust, and another boy mixed the ingredients with alcohol. Three boys sweated over the boiling vats, stirring them continuously. Somehow my great-great-grandfather secured himself the easiest job: pouring the finished product into half-pint jars.

A small additional duty for Hercule was to carry a daily sample of the tincture to Lambertine in his laboratory on the upper floor, for the chemist to check for consistency. Lambertine was in search of new concoctions that would earn him additional patents and so was usually too busy with his beakers and vials to notice when Hercule set the jar on the table. But one day in September of 1847, he happened to look up when Hercule came in. Hercule would later report that Lambertine seemed to be waiting for him; he was standing on the opposite side of the table, his eyes fixed on the door, and when Hercule entered, the red-faced old chemist, sprouting a few wiry white tufts from his otherwise bald head, sneered and licked his lips as if he were about to spring on his apprentice and gobble him up. My great-great-grandfather Hercule was justly unnerved and so couldn't be blamed when the jar in his trembling hand tipped and the tincture spilled across a letter that happened to be laid out on the table.

My great-great-grandfather liked nothing more than to recast a careless action as heroic, and that's what he did when he returned home later that day. He stood on a chair in front of his parents and younger siblings and announced that he, Hercule Fournier, had changed the course of history. He, Hercule Fournier, might as well have turned lead to gold.

He, Hercule Fournier, had risked losing his apprenticeship in order to demonstrate that the *Tinctura lambertina* had a secret property more powerful than Lambertine himself had ever guessed.

Some people are blessed with good luck, and Hercule, from what I've heard, was one of them. He certainly was lucky that day he spilled the solution across the letter Monsieur Lambertine had intercepted from the caretaker of their country estate to Lambertine's wife.

Lambertine was a jealous man by nature, and he had come to doubt his wife's virtue. He had been searching for evidence to support his suspicion and was scouring the letter from the caretaker. By the time Hercule arrived in the room, Lambertine had concluded that the letter was no more than it appeared to be: an itemized list of repairs that the caretaker would complete by the end of the month. The chemist failed to find anything obviously fishy about the letter—not on the surface, at least. And then Hercule spilled the tincture.

Even as Hercule braced for a beating, his master watched in amazement as the damp rag pulp seemed to fill with an internal light. Invisible words began appearing, as if floating up from the depths, words that had been hidden beneath a whitewash and that now emerged, ever so faintly visible, as an address at the top of the page: *My beloved Eveline*.

Eveline was Lambertine's wife. In an instant, he must have understood what he was seeing. Beneath the trivial details on the surface, the letter contained an outpouring of secret affection. The sly caretaker had covered his love letter with a wash and then written over it with details about common-place matters. He'd been doing this for a long while as a precaution, since it was understood that many of the letters addressed to Eveline would end up in her husband's hands. When Eveline received the caretaker's letter, she had only to apply a detergent to rinse away the ink on the surface, along with the whitewash, revealing the writing underneath.

Lambertine's tincture, it turned out, had more unusual properties than an ordinary detergent. While it effectively dissolved the whitewash, it preserved the surface writing on the paper and simultaneously revivified the writing under-neath. The two letters were equally visible, like a man and his shadow.

Lambertine crumpled the paper and threw it into the fire. Watching it burn, he pictured his wife's red lips pursed, waiting to be pressed in a kiss. He felt a bitter satisfaction now that his suspicions had been validated. Only after the paper had transformed into smoke and ash did he begin to consider the potential value of his chemical solution.

You would think that the librarians for King Louis Philippe would have wanted assurance that Monsieur Lambertine had conducted extensive testing of his tincture before he applied it to the parchment pages of the invaluable Codex K.E. But consider that it was a time of civil unrest, and the king had narrowly escaped several assassination attempts. Maybe the king wasn't even aware of the scholarship devoted to the codex and could not have cared less about preserving it for future generations. Or maybe the royal librarian, in his eagerness to see the earlier writing, simply forgot to ask for any guarantee.

Picture the scene with me: We're back at Lambertine's laboratory three weeks after Hercule spilled the tincture. The rain is pounding against windows; the casements give off a scent of rust that competes with the smokiness from the coals smoldering in the fireplace. Gas lamps around the room are tipped with blue-white flames. Glass and ceramic vessels are lined on shelves, labeled and plugged with corks.

Lambertine has offered his services for free, in a bid for publicity. Attending the demonstration are the librarian, several members of the Académie Française, the six apprentices, and a young maid named Bernadette, who has stopped her work to see what all the hoopla is about. She stands just inside the door holding the pole of her upended broom, her eyes dark and wondering, her lovely brown curls spilling from beneath her lace cap. Hercule, who at this point believes himself to be responsible for the momentous gathering, thinks Bernadette more interesting than a moldy book. He wants her to notice him and strains to convey, simultaneously, his importance and his desire, showing his teeth with a smile that deepens his dimples.

Oh, those Fournier dimples. Through the generations in my family, spouses who should have known better than to marry a Fournier have cursed those infatuating dimples. Poor Bernadette, who, at age fifteen, should be feeling entirely superior to a thirteen-year-old boy, at the moment is helplessly mesmerized by Hercule's precocious seductive powers. She is staring at him as he smiles at her, both of them ignoring the tension that has overtaken the room as Lambertine applies the solution to the open codex.

At the examining table, Lambertine dabs with a paint-brush. When nothing happens, he wets the brush and begins swiping more vigorously. The librarian nervously clears his throat. Soon both sides of the parchment are soaked. The men gather closer to the table, peering as the surfaces of the facing pages begin to change. Writing becomes visible, letters form words, meaning arises like a ghost, unintelligible, in a language no one present can read, but still concretely, indisputably there, the ancient text reincarnated before their very eyes.

Hercule sees none of this. For the moment, he is not even seeing Bernadette. His gaze has become fixated on a mouse that must have taken a wrong turn and now is scrambling down the doorframe, heading toward the floor.

Hercule watches the mouse. Bernadette, who is not unaware of her beauty, wonders what could possibly be distracting him from her. She follows his eyes, tips her head, sees the mouse inches away, and erupts in a scream.

The French have multiple words for *mouse*. Does Bernadette cry out, "*Une souris*"? "*Un mulot*"? Whatever she says, it is enough to startle Lambertine's audience. All attention is fixed on the maid as she attacks the mouse with her broom. The mouse leaps to the floor and flees in a panic, running in circles around the legs of a stool, hopping desperately to escape that particular kind of fury born from terror. The maid beats at the empty space behind and ahead of the mouse. The men, plus Hercule, look on in confusion. What is happening? At that moment, no one can say, no more than they could have read what appears for a fleeting second—a how-to guide for performing a miracle, perhaps instructions for raising the dead, if the old legend is correct, exposed on the surface of the parchment before disappearing under a clay-brown stain that dilates proportionally until it reaches to the edges of both pages and starts to emit a foul-smelling vapor.

The mouse slips through the opening beside a water pipe and is gone. The men glance at each other before remembering the codex. They gaze in perplexed silence at the large, uniform blotch that obscures not just the hidden writing but the biblical verses that had once graced the surface.

It will take them some time to learn that *Tinctura lambertina* had only been tested on paper, and so it wasn't discovered until too late that it had an entirely different effect on parchment and worked as a corrosive acid, causing the ancient goatskin to disintegrate.

Staring at the disfigured codex, no one in the group notices when Lambertine quietly backs away from the table. He spins around and walks out the door. He walks out of his laboratory, out of the building, out of his life. Where he goes, no one can say. He is never seen again.

Too bad for Lambertine, my great-great-grandfather would say to the little boys and girls who were the fruits of his happy match with Bernadette. Lambertine was so worried the king would have his head that he didn't bother to defend himself. But the king was too busy with his own affairs to punish an errant chemist for vandalizing a sacred book. Within a year of the destruction of the Codex K.E., revolution broke out in France, and the king abdicated to his nine-year-old grandson. As if it were somehow his own doing, Hercule would tell his children with a roar of laughter, who would tell their children, who would tell me one day, how the great king donned a seersucker suit and, under the name of Mr. Smith, hailed a taxi to drive him away from the palace.

Meanwhile, the Codex Kraos Ephrip'tus, too damaged to save and too disheartening to examine any further, was returned to its vault, where the *Tinctura lambertina* continued to do its poisonous work, until, in the end, all that was left was an empty box.

Excuse Me
While I Disappear

*I*t's huge, Dan, huge!
    Did you say huge, Harry?
I said huge, Dan!
Did you say Hickey's Used Car Barn, Harry?
That's what I was going to say, Dan, you beat me to it.
Did you say Hickey's is having a sale, Harry?
I said

Bang!

Sal Formosa's old van rang out with an asthmatic backfire as he climbed Cider Mill Lane. He was heading to his final job of the day and what would be his fifth visit to the new Dunkirk Development. In recent months, Dunkirk home-owners were discovering that the construction company had cut every corner possible. Pipes were leaking, weak foundations were already cracking, basements were flooding because of inadequate grading, and light fixtures—Sal's specialty—were falling out of ceilings. Sal was so familiar with the type of lights installed at Dunkirk that he had loaded up on a supply of the appropriate replacement sockets. The work would take twenty minutes at most, and he would be home before five.

At the bottom of the driveway, a cast-iron jockey stood holding a lantern. He was of the vintage Jocko style, with a red vest and white pants, his original black face painted over in white. The driveway curved past the figure and between the halves of the groomed lawn to the attached garage, where Sal was glad to find extra room for parking. In preparation for an easy exit, he made a K-turn and left his van with the front bumper pointing downhill.

The house was an updated Georgian model, with a brick walkway that passed a side door beside the garage before continuing on to the front door. It always confounded Sal when there were two doors from which to choose. At some houses, a side entrance with its own mudroom was clearly the preferred option for repairmen. At others—as with this Dunkirk residence—two doors sharing a walkway were equally inviting. Maybe the side door here was used as the primary entrance because it was closer to the driveway? How could Sal know?

It was his good luck that he didn't have to make a decision, for the homeowner appeared from behind the garage, a dripping garden hose in hand. "Hey, are you my savior?" he called, and before Sal could answer, the man said, throwing the hose aside and approaching, "A new day, a new problem. You must be the electrician. Welcome to Dunkirk—Repairadise, we call it. Let me tell you, we were taken. Taken! Can you guess what this monster cost?"

The question made Sal uneasy, especially coming from a stranger. It was like being asked to guess someone's age. "Houses round here...I'd wager they start in the low four hundreds."

"Start, sure, not counting the add-ons, like floors, walls, a furnace. We're stuck with a lemon. Nothing works, everything is falling apart. Last week, the roof was leaking. Yesterday the plumber was here to fix the disposal. And now you...but I'm keeping you waiting, you got a job to do, you probably want to get home to your wife. Come on in."

huge, Dan, never before in the time of history has there been a sale this huge!

Um, Harry—

Not just big, Dan—

I think you got it backward.

Not even ginormous. It's—

You know...

I know, Dan, I know, and I want our listeners to know how huge, really huge—

Harry, I think you mean in the history of time rather than in the time of history, not that it matters but—

* * *

Sal usually could predict from the look of a house how he would be treated by the owners. From the oversized hydrangeas that shone like plastic to the vinyl facade, he would have expected to be met by the brittle executive type, male or female, who called for a repair and then treated Sal with impatience, even vague disgust, as though the problem had originated with him. The owner of 37 Cider Mill Lane, in contrast, was welcoming; his friendly candor put Sal at ease as he led the way up the walk to the front door. There was even something faintly familiar about the man. Sal had a good feeling about him, as if they'd met long ago, in another context.

"Henry McCarter," the man said, extending his hand.

"Sal Formosa." Sal awkwardly bumped his belt pack against the entranceway as Henry led him inside. He straightened the buckle and then bent down, preparing to untie his boots.

"Go ahead and keep them on, Sal," Henry said, adding, "we're not clean freaks around here."

Sal's first impression of the house was that it was, in fact, freakishly clean, with sparkling wood floors, milk-white walls, and a gleaming mirror above the mantel. The two-story foyer extended into an expansive family room with panel screen doors that opened to the deck and a huge backyard. A teenage girl was sunk into the leather couch, watching a movie on her iPad. On the floor, a younger boy was building an unidentifiable structure with Legos. Neither bothered to acknowledge the electrician.

"There's the culprit," Henry said, pointing up at the chandelier. It was of a modern ebony wood variety, with linen shades and brushed nickel accents. Sal estimated the drop at fifty inches, plus the extra length added where the fixture had come loose, ripping the wires.

"That's unfortunate," Sal said.

"I'm meeting with my lawyer. We're gonna go after the contractors, I tell you. And we're not the only unhappy owners around here."

"We get a lot of complaints from this development."

"The question is, can you fix it?"

"I've fixed plenty worse."

"Sal, you *are* my savior. Hey, you thirsty, you want a beer or something? Are you allowed to have a beer when you're on a job? I mean, it's almost the end of the day. How about a beer?"

"Sure, that would be welcome when I'm done. I just gotta carry in my ladder, and I'll get going."

But what, Dan? What matters is that it's happening now, and it's the biggest sale of the summer! Did I say biggest? No, I said huge, and you are hearing about it for the first time on WHIZ 102.2. So come on down to Hickey's in Websterville and tell them you heard about the sale straight from Harry the Whiz. Now let's ask our eye in the sky for an updated weather report. Dan, what's it doing out there?

I'm looking out the window. The skies are clear and the sun is shining. Back to you, Harry.

Great news, listeners, it's sunny in Websterville. Time is 8:15, and you know what happens at 8:15, Dan!

Story time, Harry.

That's right, Dan. Are you ready for

The girl complained that she was hungry, her brother told her to shut up, she kicked at his Legos, crumbling a portion, the boy bit her in the ankle, the girl howled, and their father threatened to murder them both by vivisection if they didn't behave.

"Dad, you're gross!" The girl punched the sofa.

"What's vivisection?" the boy asked.

Henry ignored them. "You got kids?" he called up to Sal.

Sal's wrench slipped out of his hand, luckily landing on the ladder's top rung. He made a grunting sound that Henry mistook as affirmative.

"Then you know what it's like. I mean, what do you say to universal free boarding school for children ages six to eighteen! They try our patience, don't they, Sal? They think they own the world."

"Dad." The girl beat up the cushion again, this time with the top of her head.

"How does your wife handle it? I bet she is a sweetheart, you must have a nice family waiting for you at home, Sal. Not like my family. My wife's the main breadwinner. I'm a kept man, I'll say it, I'm not ashamed. The missus is a dermatologist, she makes a good living shooting up housewives with Botox. We have Botox to thank for 37 Cider Mill Lane. Does your wife do Botox, Sal? I bet she's got natural good looks. A man like you wouldn't settle for anything less."

It became apparent only gradually to Sal, as he struggled at the top of the ladder to keep his balance, huffing from the effort, his fingers deep inside the chandelier's junction box, that the man named Henry had leaped to assumptions about Sal's personal life that now would be difficult to correct. It was true that Sal had had a wife once; he'd even had a son. But his wife had moved to Arizona twenty years ago and taken the boy with her. Sal used to see the boy once a year, then once every few years, and then not at all, and so wasn't able to say goodbye when the boy, after joining the marines, was shipped to Kabul, where he was killed eight months later in an IED attack. None of this could be communicated by Sal from the top of a ladder, so he decided to keep his mouth shut. While he attached the new wire to the socket and bolted the bracket into the ceiling, he let Henry rattle on about family life. By the time Sal climbed back down the ladder, the rung locks squeaking from his weight, he found himself caught in such a thick web of presumption that there was nothing to do but play along.

a doozy, Dan?

I'm ready, Harry.

Okay, Dan, it begins like this. Me and my wife, we decide to upgrade, you see, and we're looking around for a new house, something flashy—

Nothing less than a cardboard McMansion for Harry the Whiz.

Rub it in, Dan, go ahead. So we hear about the new development at Dunkirk.

Maybe they shouldn't have called it after a battlefield, Harry.

Maybe they shouldn't have built it in the first place, Dan. Anyway, like I was saying,

Sal was not normally a liar. He viewed lying in the same realm as acting, and he was not inclined to do it without training. That said, he had always envied actors their ability to hide inside their pretend selves. He'd had a brief experience in theater as an adolescent when he was cast as a photographer in a high school production of *Anything Goes*. He had enjoyed the whole experience and especially loved popping out to the front of the stage and making the flash go off on his camera. But it was clear he didn't have the looks for a future in theater; instead he spent his later years in school working on the stage crew. That was how he got interested in wiring. Through his life, he had never lost his love of theater. Currently, he served as the volunteer electrician for the Websterville Community Theater group. He was in the audience for every show, available in case something went wrong.

Sitting at the granite island in Henry's kitchen in Dunkirk, promised beer in hand, Sal was forced to improvise. There was no gracious way to explain that he had been misunderstood when asked about his life. Instead he had to think up names for his three daughters (Sheri, Lucille, and Stacey) and give his wife, whom he called Kim, her hair color (strawberry blond). He had to come up with an excuse for not carrying photographs of his family (his wallet had been stolen—the current one was a recent replacement). As Henry opened two more beers, Sal was in the midst of inventing particular talents for his children (Sheri played volleyball, Lucille was great with computers, Stacey was taking figure-skating lessons).

With his dormant creativity tapped, Sal found that making up a family for himself was more fun than he'd expected. He told Henry that Sheri was a fearsome creature when she lost in a volleyball tournament—"You can see the steam coming out of her ears!" Sal announced. "She's like, there's no worse tragedy than losing. But I can always cheer her up by taking her for vanilla-chocolate-swirl soft serve. Cheers me up, too. Nothing like vanilla-chocolate-swirl soft serve."

"How come we never go for soft serve, Dad?" Henry's daughter called from the family room.

"You're making me look bad, Sal," said Henry cheerfully.

The two men went on talking. Sal couldn't remember another experience in his years of service when a customer had treated him completely as an equal. Henry appeared truly interested in Sal and ready to claim him as a friend. He wanted to compare their experiences as fathers and hear all about the wife named Kim. Growing ever more comfortable with Sal, Henry admitted that he was a city man at heart; he had moved to the suburbs for the schools, but one day he hoped to live in a downtown loft overlooking the river. Sal said his own dream was to have a cabin in the Adirondacks— a rustic cabin lit with kerosene lamps, he said, so he wouldn't be inclined to tinker with any wiring.

Sal felt good just whiling away what was left of the day, drinking, talking, pretending to be someone he wasn't. Usually he ended work with a quick trip to the prepared foods department of his local grocery store. He was grateful for this variation in his routine. He felt invigorated by the freedom to make up a life for himself. He was like a man who had been too preoccupied to eat and suddenly was made aware of his hunger upon seeing his favorite foods laid on the table before him. He was ravenous—emotionally, yes, and physically as well. He had been working hard all his life. It made sense, then, that after Henry's wife, the dermatologist, came home from work and invited Sal to stay for dinner, he gladly accepted.

there's this guy comes over to my house.

Who's the guy, Harry?

This guy, he comes over to fix the new chandelier. Of course the chandelier is broken because it was installed by Dunkirk.

The guy you're talking about, he's an electric guy?

Yeah, I got a light falling out of the ceiling 'cause the builders didn't install it right. So I pick up the phone and call a repair company. He's the one they send, and he comes in, and the next thing I know he's got the light fixed up, and he sees me drinking a beer. He looks at the beer like he wants one. So I offer him one. And he says yes.

Uh-oh, I think I see what's coming. The guy says yes to a beer.

He says yes.

So you give him one.

I give him one, and—

* * *

At first Sal believed that Henry's friendliness was genuine, yet he felt a gradual change in the mood during dinner with the McCarters. He couldn't identify any one comment or gesture that put him on edge, but he began to fear that the whole artificial apparatus of his fictional life was suddenly visible to his audience. Was there a slight snarl to the smile that Henry's wife flashed at him? Were the children snickering? Was there something a little excessive in Henry's curiosity about Sal's home life? Sal did his best to pretend to be a family man, but he kept worrying that he would be exposed as a bald-faced liar.

The McCarters had whipped up a fine dinner: Dr. McCarter reheated a potato casserole she'd made the previous day, and Henry threw a big T-bone on the grill, bringing it to pink perfection. Sal should have had nothing to complain about. Still, his nervousness grew as his stomach was filled. He had a sore back molar and chewed his meat with difficulty; bloody juice kept dribbling out the side of his mouth. When he blotted himself with the napkin, a pin-sized bit of paper stuck to his chin. He felt it there and rubbed it away with the back of his hand. The paper fell onto his piece of meat. Not knowing what else to do, he deliberately cut a forkful of steak and ate it, along with the bit of napkin. The boy giggled. The girl suddenly announced that she had to run to the store for something. The parents exchanged an inscrutable look as their daughter grabbed the

car keys off the counter and left the room. Sal heard the garage door opening. He could feel a tension rash sprouting on his cheeks. He could smell his own stink from a long day's work. He wondered if his awkwardness had more to do with money than the lies he had spun. Wasn't there an old saying about how the twain of rich and poor weren't meant to mingle? He wished he'd been better educated. Yet the McCarters were being generous, including him in their family dinner. If there was a source of scorn, he was it. The invented Sal was ashamed of the real Sal, he'd come to realize by the time Dr. McCarter was clearing the plates. Sal Formosa hadn't been playing a harmless little game of pretend. He had been playing a game of hide-and-seek, and he had been found—by himself. He might as well have been gazing in a mirror and seen in his reflection a man defined by his loneliness.

He felt wretched, but only momentarily. Just as he was concluding that there was nothing left to do but fess up and admit he had no family of his own, the McCarters' teen-age daughter returned. Having used her own money at the Dairy Queen, she surprised their guest with a bucketful of vanilla-chocolate-swirl soft serve.

And he drinks your beer, Harry?

He drinks it, Dan. This guy, he's got a family of his own at home, a wife and kids, and it's after five, and he's just hanging out drinking my beer. He keeps talking. He tells me all about his kids, his wife. I make a point of looking at the clock, but he won't take the hint. He gets to talking about going to volleyball games with one of his daughters. What do I care about volleyball? Then my wife comes home, she sees this stranger sitting in our kitchen drinking a beer, she waits for him to leave, but he won't leave, so what do you think she does?

Oh no, Harry. She doesn't.

Oh yes, Dan. She does. She invites the jerk to

Sal felt triumphant by the end of dinner. He was considered worthy of a trip to Dairy Queen! The lies he'd told were incidental. Of course, when Henry prepared to write a check to pay for the repair of the light fixture, Sal refused to produce a bill, saying that he couldn't accept money from friends. There was goodwill all around, especially when the McCarters were showing Sal to the door.

"This has been real special for me, thank you," Sal said.

Dr. McCarter took her husband by the hand. "Harry, you have to tell your listeners about Sal."

"Listeners?" Sal asked, though his mind was working fast. He was on the verge of guessing Henry's identity when Henry announced, "I have a little radio show, man."

"Not so little," corrected his wife. "Sal, meet Harry the Whiz."

"Sweetheart, you can't just assume Sal knows my show."

"Sure, I know it. I listen to you every day on the way to work!"

"Then maybe you noticed I'm one of those guys with a motor mouth. And I always like to give a boost to local talent. You can count on me to recommend your services on air, Sal."

So Henry McCarter was Harry the Whiz, the locally famous talk show host on Sal's favorite station. Sal might as well have discovered that he'd been dining with a king!

dinner.

Dinner? No way, Harry.

Dinner, Dan, he stays for dinner. He's there telling us about his wife and kids, and how much his daughter loves soft serve, he's telling us he gets his daughter soft serve when she loses in

As he drove away, Sal reflected on the evening. The McCarters had treated him as an honored guest. They had wined and dined him as they would have a true dignitary. They had expressed sincere interest in his life. When the wife had made a comment about upcoming state legislation, hinting that she was antiunion, Henry had come to the defense of repairmen, insisting that they were just as important as doctors. He'd gone so far as to compare electricians to neurosurgeons. "I can't imagine all you guys need to know in order to work with live wires."

By the time Sal arrived at his solitary house in Valentine, a small town in the adjacent county, he was nothing less than joyful—a feeling that lasted all through the night, infusing his dreams, and into the morning, as he headed out to his first job and tuned the van's radio to 102.2.

volleyball. It's five o'clock, then six, then seven, and he's still there in the house, Dan. He's still talking. It's like, it's dark outside, and he's never going to leave.

You're telling me he just came to fix the light, and he's still

Sal listened for a few minutes. Driving along the country road that would take him to the highway and into the suburbs, he passed a herd of deer standing in a meadow. A hawk circled overhead. A series of dump trucks sped downhill in the opposite direction, heading toward the construction site of a new development. Sal found his aching molar with the tip of his tongue. He couldn't tell whether it was his glasses or the windshield that became foggy. He raised his hand, his plump fingers hovering close to the dashboard. He kept his left hand lightly balanced on the steering wheel. His mind wandered, though not far. He reviewed the events of the previous evening and tried to come up with a new interpretation, but his thoughts kept circling unproductively around arbitrary memories from the previous day: the dripping garden hose, the clatter of the wrench, the taste of the soft serve. He glanced down at the radio.

Chugging uphill, his van let out a loud backfire, startling the deer, which looked up from the grass. Sal did not flinch and instead thought about how everyone has the freedom to make choices. No matter how unimportant you are, if you are a voting citizen in a democracy you

there, and it's dark, and you're thinking, This is friggin' weird, Harry.

The whole dinner, Dan. He stays for the salad, the steak, the potato casserole, he can't stop eating. My daughter, she's a real jokester, she goes out and gets soft serve and brings it back in a bucket. The guy loves soft serve.

So he eats it.

He eats it. This guy, he really

can choose between doing your job or neglecting it. You can choose between being a friend or a bully. You can choose between going forward or turning around and going home. When you're young you can choose to enlist in the marines or to become an electrician. If you're an electrician, you can join the International Brotherhood of Electrical Workers, though you don't have to if you don't want to, you

can pack it away, and he hasn't been working out in the gym, I doubt he's ever set foot in a gym.

Are you saying he's fat, Harry?

That's what I'm telling you, Dan, I mean, you

don't have to do anything you don't want to, not even exist another day. Existence is not an irrefutable obligation. You can veer into the path of an oncoming dump truck, or you can stay in your own lane, the same way that you can let electrons keep flowing through a wire loop or stop them merely by flipping a breaker, just like you

got to realize, this guy isn't merely big, Dan, he—

can choose between stopping the thoughts looping through your brain and, with your finger an inch away from the buttons for the radio, stopping the voices reverberating across the airwaves,

I'm way ahead of you, Harry, I know what you're going to say!
   Then go ahead and say it for me, Dan, tell our listeners what I was

though maybe not all at once, maybe turning down the volume gradually just so you know you're the one in control, you're the one doing the choosing by reducing the volume until all you can hear, before you hear nothing at all, is a pathetic whine that fades out as you reach the final rise.

Absolute Zero

A light drizzle was falling the day I pulled up to the small warehouse on Monument Road. A faded sign above the garage door indicated that the building had once housed a repair business for outboard motors. The wide tilt door was raised, leaving the interior open to the damp air. I parked my car, as I'd been instructed to do over the phone, in the lot of the old Mother of Sorrows Church across the street. My footsteps on the gravel seemed to go unnoticed, and I couldn't find a bell to ring. I had no choice but to enter of my own accord, announcing my presence as I crossed the wide threshold.

"Hello there? Mr. Farley?"

Paper sheets tinted a creamy blue were clipped to clotheslines crisscrossing the space. They hung at eye level, creating deep, latticed curtains that blocked my view of the rest of the room. They looked as thin as butterfly wings yet were firm enough to make a crackling sound as I pushed them aside.

"Hello? Anybody home?"

"Here I am!"

I headed toward the rear of the room in the direction of the voice. Parting the last row of flags, I emerged into the open space of a kitchen area, where a small, freckled man with frothy white eyebrows and a collar of a beard stood beside the stove, stirring the contents of a cauldron with a huge metal spoon.

"Mr. Farley?"

He kept stirring and stirring. I watched, transfixed. The fragrance reminded me of Elmer's paste. It must have been a thick concoction, for he was expending considerable effort just to bring the spoon around in a full circle.

"Terence Farley?"

He lifted the spoon, shaking off the drips of a gluey substance before setting it aside. He tipped the entire contents from the pot into an adjacent trough, then picked up a framed screen from a stack and dipped it into the hot stew, extracting a pulp that was a shade bluer than the rectangles. He tipped the screen to coat it, then left it to drain on a mesh counter and repeated the process with another screen.

"My record," he finally announced, "is one thousand eight hundred and two sheets in a single day—but that was with the help of three assistants. It has been a long while since I've been able to afford assistants. I've discovered that the older the cloth, the faster it drains. You can imagine my delight when I learned that the Silicon Chip factory was updating its shop coats. I offered to take the old coats for free, saving the company an expensive landfill penalty." Without looking up, he said, "You have no idea what I'm talking about, do you?"

I decided to play along. "You're making soup with shop coats?"

"Oh, you young people," he said. I wasn't sure whether I heard him chuckle or cough. He peeled off a blue skin of pulp he'd left drying on one of the screens and laid it carefully over a piece of felt. "Haven't you ever seen handmade paper before?"

"Why is it blue?"

"Because the shop coats were blue, of course. Hand me two pins."

I followed his pointing finger to a basket and dutifully fished out two clothespins for him. He hung the sheet of paper on one of the few spaces left on the rope nearest the stove.

"Now how may I help you?"

I was masquerading as a scholar with a degree in American literature and a particular interest in Terence Farley's own efforts as an author. I'd written ahead to request an interview. But something in his tone of voice made me wonder if he'd already seen through my ruse.

"I was just hoping to ask you a few questions," I said nervously. I fumbled around in my rucksack for my notebook and pen. When I tried to write the date, I discovered that the pen was out of ink. I swore under my breath, glad that Mr. Farley was turned away from me.

"See the table to your right?" he interrupted. "You'll find a pen in the drawer."

I watched him watching me as I retrieved the pen. His attention made me uncomfortable, for I could tell he was assessing my trustworthiness, though I shouldn't have been surprised.

I decided to try a different tactic. "Honestly, I am just crazy about paper. I love paper in all its forms. I love the feel of it. You know that smell when you crack the spine of an old paperback? I love that smell."

He continued working in busy silence, dipping and stacking screens. Waiting for his reply, I began to worry that I struck him as stupid.

Finally, he cleared his throat. "Did you know that there are scientists in Switzerland who are working to reverse the How Effect?" he asked. "Surely you've heard of Gerta How!" he insisted. "She was the scientist at Cambridge who perfected the process of compressing light into matter. Well, there are scientists in Switzerland today who claim to be able to turn matter into light and still preserve its informational code. That's impressive. It makes teleportation a real possibility. Sometimes it feels that we're on the verge of knowing everything there is to know."

He clipped a damp sheet of paper to the rope and picked up another screen, dipped it, and drained the liquid. His manner was efficient rather than rushed as he moved through the different components of the process. All the while, he continued speaking, almost seeming to forget he had an audience. Now and then a breeze passed through the room, rippling the sheets of paper and carrying the pungent richness of the salt marsh.

I'm not sure how long I'd stood and stared before I remembered that I was supposedly there to interview Terence Farley. He might wonder why I wasn't taking notes. I started scribbling in haste, pretending to keep up with him. I thought at the time that it would not matter what I recorded, and so I ended up with a mishmash of misspellings, nonsense, even hatched lines and doodles in place of words. Luckily, though, I have a good memory. I remember what Terence Farley told me that day, almost word for word.

"You have to understand," he said in what I thought was the beginning of a sentence but ended emphatically. *You have to understand.* He drained two more screens before he continued. "Have you ever seen a photo of a terola?" He didn't wait for me to answer. "Of course you haven't, because they've never been photographed. They are antelope-like creatures that live in the Kunlun Mountains of Tibet. They are said to be the origin of the unicorn myth, for the males sport one long, spindly horn. None exist in captivity. Some scientists believe they are on the verge of extinction, and have fought to protect their habitat. Others insist they never existed at all." He glanced at me as he secured a damp sheet to the rope. I prepared myself for what I predicted would be one of those familiar lectures about environmental stewardship so often repeated by people of his generation. Instead he asked,

"Is it worth trying to preserve a species whose existence has never been officially documented?"

I hesitated, sensing that I was being tested. "Sometimes," I said slowly, "we become aware of the extent of a loss only after it is gone forever."

"Provoking us to reconstruct it in memory." There was a hint of bitterness in his voice. "But what if it never existed in the first place?"

"At least we'll have a story to tell."

His expression softened. He surveyed me with new interest.

"I used to believe that I preferred to keep to myself," he said. "Solitude came as naturally to me as writing did. I thought I wanted to be alone—and then I met Leslie."

The tip of my pen slipped vertically down the page, but he seemed not to notice.

"I suppose I've gotten used to being alone since he died. But I don't need to tell you about his death. Death is a most uninteresting topic, with an ending that is always the same. Better is the study of origins. That's why you're here, isn't it? To find out how I got started? All right then, I'll tell you. I have nothing to hide.

"Back then I thought I was feeding on the nectar of the gods. I bought up whole boxes of paperbacks at yard sales. When I wasn't at home reading, I was in the town library reading. I just wanted to absorb every meaningful phrase that had ever been fixed in writing, whether poetry or prose. I found I relished that particular kind of concentration demanded when language is configured in such a way as to create exceptional resonance. I used to ask myself after I read a good book, What if I hadn't read it? What if I didn't even know it had been written? What if? What if!"

Transferring a sheet from the screen to the velvet, he stumbled a step, and the paper ripped and dropped from his hands. Without hesitation, he scooped up the damp clump and threw it back into the vat.

"I confess that I never had much interest in writing. All I wanted to do was read. But I felt I had an obligation to contribute my own effort to our species' vast library, so I wrote a book, just one, which, as you know because you say you've read it, lacks the resonance that raises the best of intentions to the level of art."

I thought it my duty to object and was preparing to insist that the book—which I'd only glanced at, to be honest, I hadn't bothered to read it in its entirety—was truly brilliant, but he held up his hand to silence me. "I am not ashamed to admit it was a failure. Oh, perhaps the book itself wasn't entirely to blame. Even back then, it was difficult to convince the public to read anything longer than a headline. At the same time, once accounting records could be accessed online, no one wanted to be bothered with unpopular commodities. Novels were considered particularly disgraceful. Do you know that today, every manuscript being considered for publication has to be validated through a mechanical t-test? Those that fail are labeled uninteresting nulls and returned to sender. Could you hand me two clips?"

I obliged and stood aside as he moved to hang the sheet on the rope.

"'Absolute, unproductive beauty,'" he said with a whistling sigh. "That's how Proust described an expanse of buttercups. He might as well have been describing literature. The work I care most about has little to offer in terms of utility. And so it has been suppressed through the simplest means, by being ignored. I never saw it coming. We don't need any ban on books—they disappeared on their own. My own brother, who works in the insurance industry, calls me old-fashioned. At best, he points out, there's the polluting wattage that goes into recycling. Worse is when a good, sturdy pine in Arkansas has to sacrifice its life for the sake of a few reams of paper."

For a moment I thought I heard the sound of a train easing to a stop, but it was just the flames on the huge stove licking at the bottom of the vat.

"My brother is right, of course. I am guilty of being old-fashioned. So I learned to make my own books in the old-fashioned way.

"For six months," he reminisced, "I lived in a monastery built on a hillside overlooking the River Sorgue. I slept in a stone cell on a thin mattress. I ate a sour bread made by the monks and drank the water from a natural spring so deep that no diver has ever succeeded in reaching its bottom. It was a hard life, but there must have been something magical in that water. I am sure I grew younger in those months. I learned how to make paper from a monk named Brother Jean. When I came home, I purchased an antique mill-board machine and set it up in my basement. I sharpened the blade, recalibrated the gauges, tightened the screws on the treadle, and then sent out calls. That's when I met Leslie Klavan. Maybe you've heard of him? That's Klavan with a K."

I scribbled nonsense in my notebook, faking an attempt to write the name correctly. Klavan with a K. Who? You're not talking about that writer who is so obscure that his Wikipedia page was deleted when he was deemed to be the fictitious creation of a bot? Not the author of the rarest of rare books that most book dealers have concluded never really existed in the first place, but if it did exist would be coveted by collectors around the world? Not the man who, as I recently learned, had been Terence Farley's lover?

Leslie Klavan with a K? Never heard of him, I communicated with a shake of my head.

"This is the Baskerville method I'm using, by the way," he said. I had not traveled twelve hundred miles to learn about the history of papermaking, but Terence Farley continued anyway. "John Baskerville was an English printer in the eighteenth century. He'd been trained as a headstone engraver and went on to found a successful varnishing business. He used his wealth to pursue his other passions, including papermaking. In collaboration with a friend, he developed a process that could produce smooth, wove paper using a fine wire mesh. Because the world too often fails to appreciate ingenuity, John Baskerville died penniless and was buried in a pauper's grave. He, the headstone carver, had no headstone. Yet here's the thing about John Baskerville: he may not have had wealth, but he had friends, and one friend stole his body from the grave and replanted it in a church vault, below a stone plaque inscribed with his name—though I'm not sure what all that has to do with anything."

He was searching my face again, looking for a reaction. "Oh," I said.

"*His body lies a-mouldering,*" he sang. "At any rate, his method survived him."

"And now you're using it."

"Making paper with wove paper from cast-off clothing. No tree has to give up its life for our sake. For thirty years, my job was to produce the paper used by Les for his book. In the end, I also cut the pages for his book, and bound it by hand. If you want to tell my story, you need to include Leslie Klavan."

Oh, sure, I intended to include him. My future depended on Leslie Klavan and his precious book.

"Is he still alive?" I asked gingerly, though I already knew the answer.

"Long dead. He worked as a grade-school tutor in New Britain and wrote his book in the evening. We became lovers. Then, after the accident…"

He drifted into silence without finishing the sentence. At first I thought he was so busy stirring the contents of the vat that he'd lost track of the thread of his story. As I watched him, though, I began to sense that he was waiting for something. He was waiting, I guessed, for my reply.

"What accident?"

I was fortunate that I'd found in Terence Farley a man willing to trust me. While he derived sheets of paper from factory shop coats, he went on to tell me about the drunk driver who drove the wrong way on the interstate and hit Leslie Klavan's car head-on. And he told me much more.

Over the course of the hour, he confirmed the rumor that only one copy of Klavan's book had ever been made. He also confirmed the story I'd heard that a prominent public figure who insisted on keeping his identity secret had bought the book, and then returned it after reading the first page. And he communicated another fact that I already knew: *Absolute Zero* was the title of Klavan's book.

I was rattled by the sound of the words when Terence Farley spoke them aloud. *Absolute Zero.* I aimed to make my fortune with those words, and with Terence Farley's help. But had he seen through me? Was he leading me on, batting me about between his paws, pretending that he didn't know what I was after, while I pretended to know nothing about that rarest of rare books?

In a lame attempt to show my ignorance, I tried to clarify the spelling of the title—"A-B-S—"

He interrupted. "I can't begin to describe the book. You'll have to read it yourself. It takes time, I warn you. It's a long book, necessarily so, given its scope, but it's worth the effort. There's the scene when the little girl named Jackie breaks into the hardware store in the dead of night. What a scene. And Harry Le Mont riding alone on a tandem bicycle around and around the old tarmac of the abandoned airport…"

His voice trailed off again. I forced out a cough into my cupped hand. In the most casual voice I could muster, I asked where I might find the one extant copy of Leslie Klavan's book.

"If only anyone knew!"

Terence Farley apologized for not being of more help to me. Turning off the burner beneath the vat, he said, "Les would have appreciated your interest."

After spending over an hour with Terence Farley, I gingerly asked him my final question: By any chance, did he have Leslie Klavan's original manuscript?

"Not even a page of it," he announced, suddenly cheerful.

I couldn't hide my frustration. "You made a book that was supposed to last, a book that was meant to be read by future generations. You didn't even save the manuscript?"

He shrugged. As I closed my notebook, he unclipped a sheet of paper from one of the ropes and handed it to me. "Here's a start. Maybe it will help you find what you're looking for." He gave a courtly bow.

I thanked him for the piece of paper, and for his time. I lied and promised to send him my article when it was finished. I bet he'd already guessed that I wasn't writing any article.

Back in my car, I headed up Monument Road, but instead of continuing toward Route 6 and home, I turned down Pochet Road and followed it all the way to the end. I parked and made my way along a path strewn with reeds that had been broken and blown about by the winter storms. I climbed up the rise of the dune. It had stopped drizzling, and on the other side stretched the ocean, the waves breaking in rapid succession, leaving a line of creamy froth on the shore.

I descended the dune to the beach, slipping sideways down the wet sand. The wind was stronger closer to the water. I enjoyed the feeling of my hair whipping about and the light sting of sand on my cheeks. Offshore, a trio of black-and-gray puffins bobbing like corks would have been indistinguishable from the water without their fiery plump beaks. Further out, I caught sight of the brown head of a seal. Along the edge of the surf, a single tern chased the waves, leaving a line of tiny tracks in the wet sand.

Many years earlier, I'd come on a school trip to Cape Cod, and our class had stopped somewhere near this beach at a small telegraph museum. We learned about Le Direct, a 3,200-mile-long marine cable that had been laid in the nineteenth century, connecting France to the United States. In one of the displays was a card marked with dashes and points that had been embossed by the stylus of the telegraph machine. We were told that it was a copy of the message from France announcing that Charles Lindbergh had landed safely after his flight across the Atlantic.

As a young girl, I'd been frustrated that I couldn't decipher Morse code on my own. Now, as I looked at the tracks left behind by the tern, I laughed at the thought that the lines in the sand might contain a secret message that I couldn't read. And then, on second thought, I stopped laughing.

I drove back the way I'd come, intending to see one last time the warehouse across Monument Road from the old Mother of Sorrows Church. I saw the church on one side of the road but I didn't see the warehouse. Thinking I'd missed it, I turned the car around and drove more slowly in the opposite direction. But the warehouse wasn't there. In its place was a white clapboard house with cottage-style dormers.

Had I been drugged? What happened to the worn, gray warehouse where I'd spent the hour with Terence Farley? Did Terence Farley even exist? Had he suffered the same fate as the supposedly fictitious author named Leslie Klavan, who had been expunged from Wikipedia?

I turned the car around and drove back past the church. There was the white house with peaked dormers. Where was the warehouse?

Why, the cottage *was* the warehouse, I realized at last. The building looked entirely different. The tilt door had been lowered and the light of the setting sun, which had sunk beneath the heavy cloud bank, brightened the worn facade. The faded sign was blotted in shadows cast by the overhang of the roof.

I drove back to Boston. Later that evening, alone in my hotel room, I pulled out my spiral notebook from my bag and opened to the place where I'd inserted the sheet of hand-made paper. It was still slightly damp, its edges beginning to curl. I smoothed it flat against the desk. The blank creamy blue was the limpid tint of the upper atmosphere.

You have to understand, Terence Farley had said. Understand what? Just as I'd imagined finding a message in the tracks left by a bird, now I imagined that somehow this paper contained a clue. Wouldn't it be a fine trick if the invaluable book I'd been searching for were written on this single sheet in invisible ink? Technology cast its truth in codes that were baffling to the uninitiated. Could it be that every word was squeezed on a single sheet made of repurposed rags? I stared at that perfect emptiness until my eyes burned. My longing to see impossibilities where there was nothing drove my thoughts into a knot of incoherence. Truly, I felt the limitations of my own consciousness as an oppressive physical constraint, to the point of suffocation. The blankness expanded, gathering weight, extending beyond dimension. The sensation I experienced that night is beyond any account I can offer. I don't even like to remember it. All I will say is that I saved myself by forcing my trembling hands to hold that sheet of paper at its top edge and ripping it in two, then ripping the two pieces into four and the four into eight, et cetera, until all I had left was a fistful of confetti, easily tossed from my hotel balcony and scattered every which way by the wind.

Since my visit to Terence Farley, I have found plenty of books, some of them worth more than others. But the one that would make my years of searching worth it, the book that would pay for an estate on some craggy coast, high above the floodplain, the book that contains a universe, still hasn't turned up.

Somewhere in Germantown

T here was just me enjoying a bottle of beer. I wasn't making any trouble. Me in my brother's Panama shirt, my old Buyers Picks black sneakers, my stepson's Phillies drawstring shorts 'cause we're the same height even if we don't got the same width. And in my bottle: choice hops and water brewed to perfection. I was just walking along going nowhere after Maggie told me, Get out of my sight, loser, I never wanna see you again. Like I got the Billy Penn curse. So it was just me with my bottle of beer, walking along.

Anyway, I'm crossing Vernon Park and I can't remember if I turn right or left on Greene Street, and then I'm on some street I don't recognize. I'm thinking about Maggie the whole way. I got a plan for what to say to her now, if I could just find my way back home. But I can't even tell if I'm heading east or west, and the neighborhood, you know its reputation. Just last week they found a body tied up in a tarp in the woods off Magnolia Street. TV news says the police suspect foul play. Sure, they find a dead body tied up in the woods, and the police think just maybe something stinks? Go figure.

Good thing I got my bottle of beer. Then I see this guy, he looks okay, so I cross the street to talk to him. First I think he's doing some surveying, then I see he's got a paintbrush in his hand. I forget to ask him where's Wayne Avenue 'cause I see him staring at the other side of the street. What did I miss when I was over there? I take a sip of beer and look in the direction he's looking. All I see is a building, and some more buildings.

I give a juicy burp to let him know I'm there. Watcha painting? I ask.

Those buildings, he says.

Buildings are buildings, I say. Don't look like much goes on there. Then I think maybe he's making an ad for some kingpin flipping real estate.

He goes on painting.

You just starting that picture? I ask him. It's mostly just shapes not filled in yet, and one window, and a lot of sky. But you know what he tells me? He tells me he's almost finished.

You're missing a door here, I say, touching the canvas to indicate where it goes.

Please don't, he says. I've ticked him off, but it's not more than a little smudge I've left, nothing worse than a smushed flea.

I watch him for a while. He's missing three-quarters of what's there, and he's already starting to screw the caps back on his tubes of paint. I'm bugged, you know, when a job is left incomplete. What about all those steps, and the billboards, and...? He couldn't care less. Maybe he's just bored. That gives me an idea.

How about painting *me*? I say. Come on, what is more interesting, a couple company buildings or me? I get my picture painted, Maggie will be impressed. I don't tell him that. I tell him, I got a face makes the ladies swoon. Now I'm having fun hassling him. Paint me from the neck up, how 'bout, I suggest. He's putting away his brushes. Wait, I say. I let a UPS truck go past, then I jog across the street and stand in front of the buildings. Now you get a two for one, me and your dumb buildings together, I call to him. You want to paint me in the nude, I say, that's fine. I take off my shorts and my Panama shirt. I'm down to my boxers. I can see he's looking at me, he's got a brush back in his hand. There's more, I call as I step out of my boxers. All I got on is my sneakers. I take a swig of beer. Here's a sight deserves to be immortalized. I'm on a roll. God, the beer tastes good. I want to live forever. I do a little dance, until it comes to me that I'm not making it any easier for him swishing around like this, so I stand still, not counting when I need to quench my thirst.

There I am modeling in my birthday suit when an officer of the law comes driving by. He's probably the same cop that was scratching his head when he found that body tied up and left to rot. He writes a ticket for public drunkenness and tells me to put on my clothes. I hand him my bottle of beer so I can pull up my boxers and shorts. When I'm all dressed I ask for my beer back. And you know what he does? He turns that bottle upside down and pours out what's left right in front of me, glug, glug, glug. Only then does he give me the bottle back, the fucker. I can hear him breaking up laughing as he drives away.

The painter has been watching the whole scene. I go back across the street with my empty bottle and take in his picture top to bottom, side to side. All he added since the last time I looked is blue where there used to be white inside the window. That's it. Blue nothing. I went full throttle and now I'm nowhere to be seen. Like I'm so forgettable I'm not even worth the record of my existence. A nobody. But I keep looking, and I start thinking that the blue in the window is not just any blue. It's a blue so different from the blue of the sky that it's hardly blue at all. How can I even tell it's blue if I never saw that same color blue before? I just know. It is bluer than blue, no denying, it's a real special blue, and it wouldn't be there without me. Good thing I got taste and can see I'm just what the picture needed to be perfect.

When Drummers Drum

S he is just an innocent American tourist traveling abroad
with friends, enjoying her hard-earned vacation. On the
day in question, she wakes to the aroma of fresh coffee waft-
ing up from the hotel kitchen. The geraniums in the window
box are still dripping from a refreshing rain that passed
through overnight. Now the sky is so clear that the light
sparkling on the sea hurts her eyes.

She is certain she has come to the right place to relax. If
she feels at all remorseful, it is because she has been drinking
too much of the local wine and spending more than she
can afford on clothes and souvenirs. Later in the week she
plans to take the train into the nearby city and dutifully visit
churches and museums, but today she wants to do nothing
more strenuous than climb down the stone steps to the

rocky cove, spread out a towel, and nap in the sun. In her determination to remain stress-free, she hasn't read the news since she left home.

On one side of the village, a man named Mario is drawing a razor across his chin, while on the opposite side of the village, a man named Luca is bobbing a tea bag in hot water. Though the American woman has no reason to be interested in the men at this point, they are important to this story, and I should say something about them.

The two men are the same age and as boys had been class-mates for a year, before Luca was sent off to boarding school. If Mario had let his beard grow, he would so resemble Luca that you might mistake them for brothers. That's where the similarity ends.

Mario lives in a tidy apartment overlooking a rail crossing. He enjoys the jingle of warning bells that go off every time the gates are lowered, and then the metallic churning of the passing train. His father was a carpenter, and his mother worked as a seamstress. Mario was born in an isolated hamlet in the hills, where his family had moved after his aunt was named as a collaborator in the last war and forced to endure the gauntlet of public shaming that was typical in the months following the occupation. Mario himself had never served in the military. He joined the police force as soon as he was old enough and worked his way up the ranks to the position of captain. At the age of forty-two, he finally proposed to a woman after learning that she was pregnant with his child, but she turned him down. Though he hasn't heard from her since she moved away from the village, he has no regrets. As he likes to say, it's when a man marries that his troubles begin.

Luca lives in a villa perched on a high plateau terraced with private gardens overlooking the sea. A stretch of train tunnel runs beneath this portion of the village, and the rumble as the train emerges above ground sounds like distant thunder. The villa is filled with fine art, including a small unsigned oil portrait that is said to be by Rubens, and a set of sixteenth-century engravings by Cristofano Bertelli. Luca's family is one of the richest in the region thanks to a great-grandfather who made a fortune in the sugar trade. Luca is lucky to be able to live off his inheritance and devote himself to a literary career that brings him personal satisfaction, despite the lack of public recognition. His wife, born and raised in London, works as a lawyer for an international trade corporation. They have two young children who attend the same Swiss boarding school where their father was educated, and his father before him.

Here we are, then, in a typical Mediterranean village, sometime between the end of the last world war and shortly before the next one begins. There's no obvious reason to think trouble is imminent. In the eyes of an ordinary tourist, everything looks lovely: the colorful, lopsided buildings packed on hillsides above the sea, the slopes lined with abundant vineyards and olive groves, the flowery vines spilling over fences. How could anyone not be happy here?

* * *

Luca's teacup rattles on the saucer as the train snakes deep inside the earth below his villa. He tosses his tea bag into a garbage pail and goes on writing.

On the other side of the village, the warning bells at the railway crossing start jingling. When the train roars between the gates, the engineer lets out an abrupt warning toot, ignoring the local prohibition against unnecessary disturbances and causing Mario to flinch and nick himself with the razor. He presses a tab of toilet paper against his chin to stop the bleeding.

In the village center, the cobbled streets begin to pulse with life: a woman pushes a baby carriage along the sidewalk, a man revs the engine of his motorcycle, and a butcher raises the metal portcullis over the door. Down on the beach, a small dog barks at the waves.

The American woman and her friends emerge from their hotel and wander leisurely. They admire shoes on display in a shop window. They enjoy the fragrance of fresh pastries that drifts from the open window of a bakery.

The American woman doesn't speak the local language and so cannot understand what the old women are whispering as they walk arm in arm on their way to the market, or why the old men huddled in the village square keep looking nervously over their shoulders. She is unable to read the incendiary messages on posters that were pasted on walls under the cover of night and are destined to be ripped down before noon. She is made a little uneasy by the unemployed young people lounging in doorways, who watch the Americans with surly gazes, but she figures it's just their leather jackets and the enveloping haze from their cigarettes that makes them look so tough.

In Mario's line of work, the most confidential messages are delivered by hand during the night. He is pleased to find an important one waiting for him when he arrives at the prefecture. Though the message is brief, he takes his time reading it. The deputy stands facing him across the desk, waiting for direction, but Mario is silent. The deputy clears his throat in a deferential signal of impatience. Mario extracts two cigarettes and offers one to the deputy. When the two men lean toward Mario's lighter, they look as though they are going to meet in a kiss.

The deputy mimics his boss's rhythm of smoking, blowing smoke from the corner of his mouth. Encouraged by Mario's friendly manner, he asks, "What's the news from the Capitol?"

Mario flashes his bleached teeth in a smile, and the deputy takes a step back, as if from a fire that has spit out a spark. He nods toward the paper on Mario's desk. "The message, sir?"

"A man without enemies has been forgotten by fortune," Mario murmurs, greeting the deputy's expression of confusion with another flash of his teeth. He doesn't exactly dislike the deputy, but he wishes the young man weren't so sloppy and doltish. At least the deputy has never given Mario reason to doubt his loyalty. That's important in an age like the present, when espionage has reached such a level of sophistication that one must assume adversaries have infiltrated government at the highest levels.

Mario turns the message facedown and runs the tip of his index finger over the paper to feel the back side of the official watermark. It's not every day that he receives an important communication from the president himself. Granted, he knows that the same message was sent out to all municipalities, but that doesn't mean it's any less special.

He guessed what is coming and has been looking forward to this day more than he will ever admit, though he is careful not to be distracted by an illusory gratification before he has even carried out his duty.

"Ugo," he says sharply to the deputy, grinding out the cigarette he has hardly smoked.

"Sir!" The deputy drops his own cigarette onto the concrete floor, leaving it to burn, and snaps to attention.

"I need you to set up the loudspeakers. And tell Sylvio to gather the Academy Band. We're going to have a parade, and we need music. Most of all, we need drummers. You know what they say about drummers, Ugo?"

"What's that, sir?"

"When drummers drum, the law is silent."

Meanwhile, Luca is at his desk, writing. He writes with a No. 2 pencil on lined paper. He is almost at the end of his novel and has filled a fat binder with more than eight hundred pages. Handwriting is essential in his process, for it gives him a sense of timelessness. Revision will begin when he transfers the text to his computer.

He is too deeply engrossed to worry about the merit of the work or to wonder what readers will make of it. He doesn't need to imagine the fate of the completed book. He prefers to concentrate on bringing it to life and giving it form in the shape of words that emerge so rapidly from the tip of his pencil that he can hardly keep up with them.

The novel tells the story of a Sudanese girl who at the age of eighteen sets out with hundreds of other desperate people on the perilous journey across the sea in an inflatable boat. The boat capsizes, and scores of passengers drown. The girl survives by clinging to a Styrofoam cooler. After two days in the sea, she is saved by the coast guard. She is delivered to a village much like the village where Luca and Mario live. She finds a job working as a maid in a hotel much like the hotel where the American and her friends are staying. She learns the language of the country from watching television. Halfway through the novel, she meets a boy from the village, and they fall deeply in love. Unbeknownst to them, the owner of the hotel has been plotting to sell the girl into slavery. Two thugs arrive in her bedroom in the middle of the night with the aim of kidnapping her. They find her in bed with the boy from the village, and in the scuffle they fatally stab the boy. By the time the police arrive, the thugs have fled the scene, and the girl is covered with blood. She is charged with the murder of the boy and after a trial that extends for several chapters of the book, she is found guilty and sentenced to death.

Luca is in the process of writing the last chapter, when the girl is alone in her prison cell on the final night of her life. He has given this portion of the book over to the girl's thoughts, immersing himself in their heaving, jarring movement. He feels the force of her mind affecting him physically, as if he were experiencing an accident in slow motion. With each word, he is spun and bumped, turned upside down, dragged backward, blown into the air. He can barely endure imagining the very tragedy that he has conceived. The poor, poor girl. Another writer would concoct a reprieve for her in the final pages. Not Luca. He desperately wants to save her, but he can't, or won't, because her destiny has been determined by factors laid out earlier in the book and now are impossible to change. The point is that the innocent girl must die. The community will subject her to its twisted justice, despite the author's reluctance to allow it.

He is reminded of poignant lines he recently read in a biography of the poet Rilke. The quote came from a young woman Rilke knew: "I know I shall not live very long," the woman wrote in her diary, "but I wonder, is that sad? Is a celebration more beautiful because it lasts longer?"

Luca has written his novel in celebration of a girl who is destroyed by a community's ignorance. No matter that the girl in his book doesn't exist. She is real enough to Luca to blur his eyes as he faces with her, through her, the reality of impending death. She will die. He will die. With every breath he takes, he depletes his allotment of life, until, one day, there will be nothing left. He expects that in the end he will be reduced to kicking and sobbing and calling for mercy, for he lacks the courage shown by the girl in his novel. Though she won't be spared, she will triumph by the sheer force of her independent will. She will not allow herself to descend to the depravity of those who have condemned her. She will refuse their invitation for false repentance. She will draw her fingertip along the wall as she flies from her cell into the secure refuge of her mind, marveling at the riches that are her memories and the purposefulness of her existence. To the last second of her conscious life, she will prove with the fierce intensity of her intelligence that she is free.

Round about noon, the village reverberates yet again with that familiar low rumbling that comes from having a major rail line run through the town. Down at the cove, where the American woman and her friends are sunbathing, the noise is barely audible over the gentle churning of pebbles being dragged forward and back by the waves. She lazily attributes the sound to one of those long freight trains bringing lumber down from the mountains.

In fact, there is no train this time. The crossing gates remain raised, and the traffic has come to a standstill to let a military convoy pass. Little paper flags magically appear in the hands of children, who wave merrily at the jeeps, then at the trucks packed with soldiers, and then at the trailers heaped with spanking new missiles and cannons.

Though the Americans don't know this yet, it is not unusual for a convoy to roll through the streets on its way south. The government likes to extend its show of strength beyond the cities, and this village happens to be on a route between two strategic ports. The residents feel a mix of annoyance and patriotic pride at the inconvenience. The young people in doorways look on with interest. Some of the old men even make the stiff-armed salute that until recently was considered taboo because of its association with a defeated regime and a disgraced dictator.

On one side of the village, Mario waits on the top step outside the prefecture. Clouds float in mirror images across the disks of his sunglasses. His deputy slouches nearby, resting his elbow on the butt of his machine gun. They hear the pop of a backfire. By the time the single truck full of soldiers peels away from the line and pulls in front of the building, the deputy is standing straight and tall.

On the other side of the village, Luca has paused in his work and is remembering the story his father told about how he was forced to wait along the roadside for the dictator's convoy to go past. His father, a young boy at the time, was supposed to salute; he wanted to refuse but to do so would have endangered not just him but his whole family. The boy had a clever solution: he raised his arm, but instead of keeping his hand open, he curled his fingers into his hair. For the rest of his life, Luca's father could say that instead of saluting the dictator, he only scratched his head.

The American woman and her friends are disappointed when they arrive at the little pizzeria on the terrace above the beach and find it closed. They are reduced to a lunch of tuna sandwiches on soggy, crustless white bread at a nearby café. The woman shares her friends' frustration at having to wait out the siesta to go shopping. She agrees that the country's struggling economy would improve if only the stores would stay open all day.

The sea breeze has weakened, the air is stifling, washed-up piles of jellyfish are rotting on the beach, the sun is scorching. There is nothing to do. Whose idea was it to come to this wretched village anyway? The group would have started squabbling just to pass the time if they hadn't heard the sound of brass instruments in the distance, followed by the merry beating of drums. Is it a wedding? A fair? Whatever is going on, it's sure to be entertaining.

They hurry off in the direction of the sound, winding uphill through the narrow streets until they come to the main square, where they are delighted to find a large, festive assembly. The band is playing, and the church doors are wide open. Uniformed men and women standing shoulder to shoulder are crisply outfitted and as stone-faced as store mannequins. Some of the older men in the crowd wear quaint tricorne hats decorated with a single feather. Small dogs run underfoot, chased by squealing children. When a bouquet of balloons is released into the sky, the woman and her friends all reach for their cell phones, keen to make a visual record of the experience.

The woman watches as the colorful balloons rise and separate. The trumpeters abruptly stop playing. The crowd responds with a respectful silence. For a moment, only the precise cadence from the drummers can be heard. Then even the drummers stop, and everything seems to freeze, as if locked inside a still frame of the video she has been taking, until, all at once, the whole scene shatters as machine guns belonging to soldiers the woman hadn't even noticed explode in rapid fire.

Her heart skips a beat and she drops her phone; she feels one of her friends stumble sideways and bump against her. Her first panicked assumption is that she is being gunned down, until she sees the bits of colored Mylar dropping from the sky and realizes that the machine guns had been aimed at the balloons.

The crowd erupts in cheers, and the children start running around again, racing to collect pieces of balloons. The woman and her friends share the forced laughter meant to disguise the relief following their mistaken impression. She scrambles to grab her phone before it is crushed underfoot. When she looks up again, she finds that the crowd has shifted and relocated to open a space within it, and she ends up in the front row, her view of the proceedings unimpeded.

When the police sedan pulls into the paved turnaround below the gatehouse and starts honking, Miranda, the housekeeper, leans out the upper-story window.

"Stop the racket!" she shouts. She is famous in the village for her sharp tongue and haughty manner. Some believe that she is of Romany descent; shopkeepers say she has the thieving guile of a Gypsy. She was taken into Luca's family when she was a teenager and has worked at the villa ever since; when she married, her husband was hired as a gardener, and when her two sons came of age they were placed by Luca's wife in well-paid positions in the accounting department of her corporation. Miranda repays the family's loyalty with her own. And while she can't know exactly what the police have come for, she can tell when the driver lays his hand on the horn again that they are up to no good. If *good* was their intention, the driver would have stepped out of the car instead of honking the horn; he would have taken off his cap in deference and given Miranda a polite greeting before requesting entrance.

She pulls the shutters closed, and instead of pressing the button that would open the gates, she hurries downstairs and across the yard to the back door of the main villa.

"The police are here," she hisses as she flies past the kitchen, where the cook is stirring a pot, reducing a fish stock to a savory syrup. "The police are here," Miranda hisses to the cook's little son, who is in the hallway dangling a piece of string in front of a kitten. "The police are here," Miranda announces as she throws open the door of the library without knocking, causing Luca to lose control of his pencil just as he is crossing the *t*, causing the line to veer up at an angle, cutting across the sentence above it.

Miranda's plump chest heaves as she stares at Luca. Luca blinks in confusion. Outside, they can hear the angry wailing of the car horn.

"Where are the children?" Luca asks.

"They are in Lausanne," Miranda reminds him.

"Of course, of course, what was I thinking…and Jenny?"

"She's at work."

"That's good, yes, it's normal, and the police…they are looking for me, then?"

"They didn't say."

They didn't need to say. No explanation is necessary. Luca doesn't need to be told about the slow, inexorable shift in public sentiment. He knows that those who fail to produce bald propaganda are regularly denounced as traitors and subjected to prosecution. He has been expecting the authorities to come for him for so long that he almost forgot them. Now he is faced with the choice he was unable to make in the abstract: he must agree to suppress all his work and never write another word, or else he must go into exile. If he chooses the latter course, what will become of his wife and children? If they join him, they will be forced to live an impoverished, fugitive existence for the rest of their lives. If he leaves them behind, they will suffer the repercussions of his cowardice, in his place.

He neatens the pages on his desk, stacking them in a uniform block. In a symbolic gesture whose meaning he is sure the police captain will understand, he sets his reading glasses on top of his unfinished manuscript. He pushes his chair from his desk.

"Miranda, would you tell the police, please, that if they want to talk with me, they can find me in the rose garden?"

The brown of her eyes has the particular depth of pigment you can only find in the eyes of people who are very old, when the whites around the irises have dulled. She gives a slight nod that to anyone else would indicate merely her willingness to follow a direction but to Luca communicates her fierce desire to protect him.

He puts on the white silk smoking jacket with gray cuffs that used to belong to his father. The door to the terrace opens reluctantly. Luca must add the pressure of a kick to the initial nudge from his shoulder. He leaves it ajar behind him. As he follows the stone path, he rehearses in his mind whole sentences that he will never go on to write. He has no regrets in the wake of his surrender, though at the same time he cannot hold back his tears. His cheeks are wet as he continues down the uneven path. He resists the urge to return to the terrace and listen through the open door, so he doesn't have the opportunity to hear the crunching thump Mario makes when he crushes Luca's reading glasses with his fist.

Drummers drum, trumpeters trumpet, colored confetti rises in bursts and settles into the cracks between the paving stones. The American woman and her friends are charmed by the festival and pleased with their good luck at having come upon it by accident. The surrounding buildings are tall enough to cast cooling shadows. As if to join the fun, a refreshing breeze picks up. The beautiful children, brown and limber, chase one another in a game of tag. The round, curious eyes of a long-haired Chihuahua peek out from a pocket of a young man's backpack. At the far end of the piazza, the stones come to an end abruptly, and the terraces below are hidden from view, giving the illusion that they are on a cliff high above the sea.

The music stops abruptly, and only then does the woman notice the uniformed men who have taken their place on the stage of the band shell. One of them begins speaking into a microphone, causing the sound system to erupt in a piercing squeal. He taps the microphone and tries again, counting in his language, "One, two, three"—that is all the woman can decipher of the speech that follows, a long speech delivered in the dutiful manner that suggests nothing unexpected is being revealed. She and her friends fiddle with their phones, trying to use what little broadband service there is to post their pictures on Facebook. She is glad when the speech is over, and the band begins playing again, and the musicians leave the stage and proceed across the piazza. She joins them, following the people, who are following the men in uniform, who are following the musicians.

She has no way of knowing, of course, that the procession is traveling along the same route that Mario's aunt took after being revealed as a collaborator in the aftermath of the last war. She cannot know that as Mario walks in the procession he is remembering the stories he's been told about his aunt, who was stripped naked, her hands bound, her head shaved, and was dragged by a rope around her neck down the middle of the street. His mother told him that collaborators were given laxatives before they were paraded in front of the people, but she never said what the collaborators had done to deserve their punishment.

History is what happens in books the American woman does not have the time to read now that she is gainfully employed in a field that requires an exhausting amount of attention to numbers. She is clever when it comes to analytics, she likes the work, and she has earned her vacation. She cannot be blamed if she does not understand the purpose of the procession she is marching in, or why she ends up on the public beach, or who lit the bonfire that is crackling on the sand.

To be honest, I don't speak the local language much better than the American and her friends do, and I would have been just as confused as they were that day if I hadn't happened to meet a man who knew Luca's wife. It was from him I learned about Luca and Mario, their families, their pasts, their work, and the bonfire that broadcast the wide reach of the government's crackdown on dissent and announced the end of Luca's career.

All the American knows when she is in the midst of the scene is that a pile of broken wooden chairs and crates, twigs, newspapers, old shoes, driftwood, and dried-up jellyfish carcasses has been set alight. The flames lick at the cloudless sky, reaching toward the sun. Scattered applause breaks out as into the fire is emptied a box full of papers whose significance the woman cannot guess. But she can imagine. She can't keep herself from imagining. It is mysterious, since she is necessarily so clueless, that as she watches the pages curl and dissolve into ash and smoke, the enormity of the loss stirs in her an overwhelming awareness.

Acknowledgments

I am grateful to the editors and staff who gave these stories their first home in the following journals: *Black Clock, Conjunctions, Imagistic, Puerto del Sol, Ocean State Review, The Yale Review*. "Excuse Me While I Disappear" was reprinted, under the title of "Whimper," on Lit Hub. "Principles of Uncertainty" was reprinted in *Porous Boundaries* (University of Manchester Press). Thank you to Bill Henderson and the editors for including "The Knowledge Gallery" and "Infidels" in the *Pushcart Prize* anthologies. Special thanks to Bruce Bauman, Steve Erickson, and Brad Morrow, who with their innovative writing and creative prompts fire up my imagination. And a big thanks to students and colleagues at the University of Rochester for keeping me on my toes.

Thank you to Reagan Arthur, Michael Pietsch, Jean Garnett, Betsy Uhrig, Albert LaFarge, and all at Hachette who have transformed this collection into a book and helped it reach readers.

Acknowledgments

I am grateful to the Bogliasco Foundation and the James Merrill House committee for life-changing gifts of residencies, providing me with crucial time, along with beautiful settings and new friendships.

Geri Thoma, steady beacon for four decades—thank you.

Jim, Kathryn, Alice—thank you for making it all possible.

About the Author

Joanna Scott is the author of twelve books, including *Arrogance* and *Various Antidotes,* both PEN-Faulkner finalists, *The Manikin,* a finalist for the Pulitzer Prize, and *Follow Me,* a *New York Times* Notable Book. Her awards include a MacArthur Fellowship, a Lannan Literary Award, a Guggenheim Fellowship, and the Rosenthal Award from the American Academy of Arts and Letters. Scott is the Roswell Smith Burrows Professor of English at the University of Rochester.